BRIDES OF WILDCAT COUNTY

WILDCAT COUNTY

DANGEROUS: SAVANNAH'S STORY

BRIDES
OF
WILDCAT COUNTY

DANGEROUS:
SAVANNAH'S STORY

JUDE WATSON

Aladdin Paperbacks

Copyright © 1995 by Jude Watson
Aladdin Paperbacks
An imprint of Simon & Schuster
Children's Publishing Division
1230 Avenue of the Americas
New York, NY 10020
All rights reserved, including the right of
reproduction in whole or in part in any form
First Aladdin Paperbacks edition September 1995
Designed by Randall Sauchuck
Manufactured in the United States of America
10 9 8 7 6 5 4 3 2 1
Library of Congress Cataloging-in-Publication Data
Dangerous : Savannah's story / Jude Watson. — 1st Aladdin Paperbacks ed.
p. cm. — (Brides of Wildcat County)
Summary: Seventeen-year-old Savannah escapes from an arranged
marriage to a Southern plantation owner, changes her name, and
begins a new life in a gold mining town in California.
ISBN 0-689-80326-5
[1. Gold mines and mining—Fiction.
2. Adventure and adventurers—Fiction. 3. California—Fiction.]
I. Title. II. Series: Watson, Jude. Brides of Wildcat County.
PZ7.W32755Dan 1995
[Fic]—dc20 95-15702

BRIDES OF WILDCAT COUNTY

DANGEROUS: SAVANNAH'S STORY

CHAPTER ONE
In Which a Bride Escapes Her Duty

Whoever said that all brides are beautiful hadn't met Shelby Amelia Bruneau Calhoun. Although the girl was reckoned the belle of the county, her usually blooming face was white and pinched. Even Shelby's favorite aunt, Ursula, had been heard to say that they should all be grateful for the bridal veil.

Upstairs and alone at last, Shelby collapsed onto her bed. With a savage motion, she kicked off her satin wedding slippers. She was crushing her wedding gown, but she didn't care. Fashioned from the finest watered silk, it had sixteen flounces and twenty-seven blue velvet forget-me-nots embroidered on the bodice and sleeves.

Shelby pinched one of the silk flowers along the neckline between her fingers. With a satisfied grunt, she tore it off with her teeth. She threw it into her chamber pot.

She hated her wedding dress. She hated her wedding reception. And, most important, she hated her bridegroom.

She stood up abruptly, but there was nowhere to go. Soon Mr. Justus Calhoun would be heading upstairs from the reception. Bourbon on his breath, self-congratulation in his smile. Shelby had grown up in the country. She had an idea of what lay in store for her. Her father bred horses, and once, against his strict orders, she had sneaked behind a tree to watch. The thought of the stranger heading her way made her blood run cold.

How had this happened to her? Despite being kicked out of three female academies in nine months, she hadn't truly been bad. She hadn't tried to elope or joined an abolitionist society. And she hadn't been in nearly as many scrapes as her older brother Cole, who was a gambler and on his way to becoming a drunkard.

Was it her fault that the Kincaid brothers had challenged each other to a duel over her affections? And just because she talked six girls at Miss Temple's Seminary for Young Ladies into posing for the art tutor in their shifts, did that mean she should be expelled? They were posing as Greek goddesses after all—were they expected to wear their cloaks and bonnets?

And it wasn't *she* who asked handsome Harry Delaney to charm his way into her aunt's parlor in Savannah and remain, despite the fact that they were without a chaperon. Was she expected to throw him out in the street?

But that tiny incident had been the last straw for her father, Winston Moxley Bruneau. Shelby had been labeled "fast" by the nasty tongues in Savannah, and she had been ordered home in disgrace. Just when she'd managed to get away from home for six whole, glorious months!

Shelby winced, remembering the beating her father had administered with his thick leather strap. She'd had welts on her legs for weeks.

But there were worse things in store. The next thing she knew, her father had calmly informed her that he was done with her. From now on, she would be another man's property. At only seventeen, she was engaged to be married to Mr. Justus Calhoun. She had seen him once at a county barbecue and hadn't thought him interesting enough to flirt with. More important to her father was Justus's plantation, Summer Glen, and his large income.

She had tried her best to resist. She had wailed and shrieked and cried and begged. Even after her father had locked her in her room for two weeks, she'd refused to budge. She threw the ring Mr. Calhoun sent across the room. She refused all food for three days. But then her father had kicked down her door and poured broth down her throat, and, sputtering and weeping from weakness, she had given in.

Shelby's lace-mittened hands clenched into fists. Her dark blue eyes, eyes that had been compared to a lake at twilight by romantic Harry Delaney, glittered with hard fury. She had been delivered like a prize horse. It's a wonder Justus Calhoun hadn't run a hand down her flanks or checked her teeth! And soon, she thought, shuddering, he would be doing worse to her.

He would be coming upstairs any moment. She was running out of time.

Gathering her courage, Shelby reached into the drawer of the small table by her bed. Her fingers closed around a small glass bottle.

Last night, it had taken all her courage to sneak out of the house at midnight. Keeping to the shadows, she'd gone to the quarters and knocked on the door of the kitchen maid, Lyddie. Lyddie was a midwife and had a reputation as a healer.

Lyddie hadn't even looked surprised when Shelby had whispered what she wanted. Her handsome bronze face remained expressionless, and she hadn't spoken a word until Shelby had finished her request. Lamplight lit her extraordinary liquid eyes as she gave one short nod.

"I'll see what I can do to help to help you, Miss Shelby," she'd said. And that was all.

Half a promise. All during her wedding day, Shelby had fretted. She'd wondered and worried and thought of running away. But then, as Lyddie passed her in the hallway, she'd slipped a small bottle into Shelby's hand.

Now the bottle felt slick against Shelby's damp palm. She was starting to perspire. Not wanting to delay another second, Shelby tilted back her head and drank every drop. She winced at the bitter taste.

As soon as it was down, she began to worry. What if Lyddie had given her poison? Papa was always saying that the slaves were out to poison them. But Papa said all manner of fool things, Shelby thought wryly as she lowered herself into the rocking chair.

She didn't have to wait long.

By the time the knock on the door came, she was woozy and damp with perspiration. The motion of the rocker had made the sickness worse, and she now had her feet firmly planted on the floor to keep it still.

Maybe I am dying, she thought woozily. *I've never felt so terrible in my life. I wish I could die.*

The knock came again, more insistent this time.

"Come in," Shelby croaked.

She heard the sound of the door opening. The sound of boots thudding against the floor. Shelby wasn't capable of speech. She couldn't even look up. The floor seemed to rise up and settle back down, like waves in Savannah's harbor.

He walked toward her. She could only see the tips of his polished boots. She smelled bourbon, and her stomach rolled over. Nausea shimmered through her body, and she squeezed her eyes shut tighter, willing away the dizziness. She coughed and felt sicker.

"Shelby, honey—"

The tide rolled in again. There was no time to make a dash for the chamber pot. With a most unladylike gagging sound, Shelby leaned over and deposited her wedding supper on her bridegroom's new boots.

CHAPTER TWO
A LAND WITHOUT FATHERS

She didn't die, but for one whole day she felt as if she were sure to. By the second day, she thought she might possibly recover. By the third, she was faking.

Shelby stretched as the bright sunlight poured through the curtains and made a square of gold on the carpet. She felt weak but marvelous. She'd never appreciated how wonderful it was to sleep alone in her very own bed.

As long as Winston Bruneau wasn't in a rage, life at the plantation was easy. Though Mama was active from morning till night, Shelby slept late and often breakfasted in bed. Her domestic duties were confined to tatting lace and embroidering pillows, which she was never very good at. Even during periods of domestic crisis, like the yearly hog slaughter and smoking, when her mother rose at dawn and went to bed after midnight, Shelby remained at leisure.

What she had never realized was that the reason she'd been allowed such leisure to visit, to rest, to plan her wardrobe, was simple: The purpose of her life was to catch a husband. All that time she'd been bestowing smiles and occasional forbidden kisses, she had been for sale. And now that she was married, she would not be allowed such freedoms again.

As the wife of a planter, she would work herself to the bone. She would be in charge of the provisions, the garden, the smokehouse, the dairy, and the physical well-being of all the workers. She would be mixing medicines, making quilts, salting pork, mending clothing, dipping candles, hooking rugs.

And she would, at all times, no matter how overworked, be gracious and perfectly groomed. And if her husband gambled or drank, she was expected to wait up for him. If he took a slave as a mistress and fathered children, she was expected to turn away her eyes.

She wanted none of it. She wanted to be young. She wanted to have adventures. She wanted to keep dancing.

Shelby frowned, thinking. If all went well, she could spin this illness out for a few weeks. She could plead a delicate constitution. Would Mr. Calhoun get tired of waiting and go back to his plantation? Would she be able to delay joining him for very long? Perhaps she could maneuver the doctor to say she needed sea air, and wrangle a trip to Aunt Ursula's. . . .

Suddenly Shelby heard heavy familiar footsteps approaching her door. She shrank back against the pillows as her door flew open. It hit the opposite wall with a crash.

Winston Moxley Bruneau stood in the doorway. His light brown eyes flashed as he took in the sight of his daughter. In his hand was a riding crop. He tapped it against his shiny black boots.

Shelby struggled to sit up. "I'm feeling a bit better today, Papa—"

He strode across the room and ripped the quilt off her shoulders.

He leaned over and fixed his gaze on her face. "You might think you can fool that idiot husband of yours and your sainted mother, but you can't fool me, miss. You'll get up and do your duty, by God, or there'll be hell to pay!"

Shelby's chin came up. "I *was* ill—*am* ill, Papa, truly—"

He slammed the riding crop down on the pillow next to her cheek. "You hush your mouth!" he raged. "I've seen your tricks and your lies and your cunning ways, and I won't be taken in by any of them!"

Shelby shook with fear. She saw her mother appear in the doorway. The house servants lurked behind. It was a familiar scene. Shelby saw her mother's frightened eyes and the cool-eyed glance of Opal, her mother's young personal maid.

Without turning, her father roared, "Go about

your duties before I take this crop to the back of your legs, too!"

Her mother hurried away, Opal behind her. Regina Bruneau would never interfere when her husband was in a rage. Afterward, she would slip into Shelby's room with a cool cloth and murmur how sorry she was.

"You don't own me anymore," Shelby told her father coolly. "Mr. Calhoun does now. Remember?"

She saw the struggle on his face. He would love to bring the crop down on her legs the way he had countless times before. But if he marked her, Mr. Calhoun would know.

"Get dressed," he hissed. "I want you out of my house today. I won't be disgraced by the likes of you. You'll do your duty and go with Mr. Calhoun this very morning."

Weak from lying down for three days, Shelby slid out of bed. As she used the bedpost to haul herself to her feet, she vowed that this would be the very last time she obeyed her father.

Her mother sent Opal to her to help her dress and pack. The girl would be coming with her to Mr. Calhoun's plantation. She had been a wedding present from Shelby's mother.

Shelby didn't speak as Opal tightened her stays, laid out her stockings, pinned up her hair. Opal was the color of coffee halfway mixed with thick cream. Her large, caramel-colored eyes were lighter than her mother Lyddie's, but they held the same stillness. The two girls had played together as children, but with the troubles with the Northern states her father had forbidden her friendships with slaves. The family was to speak to inferiors only to give orders.

Shelby wondered if Lyddie had told Opal about the potion she'd drawn up for her. If she knew what Shelby had done, Opal gave no sign. She brushed, smoothed, buttoned, and tidied in silence.

Then, as Opal flattened the lace edging of Shelby's new black traveling costume, she met Shelby's gaze in the mirror. Opal quickly dropped her eyes, but not before Shelby saw the knowledge in them. She knew.

"That's enough, Opal," Shelby said, twisting away from the capable fingers. "Do stop fussing. You can go downstairs and say your good-byes to your mother. I'll be down directly."

Opal nodded and left as silently as she came.

Shelby closed her trunks. She heard her father shouting at a servant in the yard to bring the carriage around. She took one last look at her bedroom. She had never really been happy here. She didn't know why she was so reluctant to leave it.

Shelby started down the polished oak floor of the upstairs hall. She composed her face into a mask of delicate suffering. Just because her father saw through her didn't mean her husband would. Perhaps she could keep him out of her bed for a few weeks if she pretended to be weak.

Unless he's a brute like Father . . .

Shelby stopped stock still with the thought. Why did she think she was so clever? What was she doing, playing possum? She was behaving like a child, inventing an illness to escape a disagreeable task. But she was not dealing with children. She was dealing with men.

She could not face her husband yet. She could not face any of them. Not her father with his cruelty, nor her mother, her mute eyes begging Shelby not to make a fuss. Not her own brother, bored with her antics and only too happy to see the back of her disappearing down a road.

She was alone. She had always been alone, she realized for the first time, standing in the upstairs hall she knew so well. She could close her eyes and picture every nick in every board, every spindle in the banister. But she didn't belong here any more than she belonged with Mr. Calhoun. Why was she searching for comfort here?

Blindly, she opened the nearest door and slipped inside. It was the second-best company room, dim and silent on that June morning. Someone had left a window open to air the room, and she sat down on the edge of the bed and took deep breaths while she tried to compose herself.

She wanted to run. But where could she go? Everyone in the county knew her. No one would take her in. They would give her a meal and plenty of smiles, but they would send her right back to her father.

There was no place for her. She didn't want to be Justus's wife, but she didn't want to be her father's daughter, either.

"Shelby Amelia! Your husband is waiting!"

Her father's bellow reached her from the downstairs hall. Shelby stood up reluctantly. There was nothing left to do but go down.

She headed for the door, but her eye was caught by something wedged between the dresser and the wall. Shelby reached over and pulled it out. It was only a newspaper, probably left behind by a wedding guest. Mother's cousin Philip Otterly, a Yankee, had come down for the wedding and stayed an unheard of short three days. Usually guests at a plantation stayed two weeks at the very least. But what did you expect from a lawyer from New York?

Shelby scanned the headline. Nothing important. More talk of government compromise and abolition. If there was one thing that bored Shelby to tears, it was politics. Her mother spent her days in a nervous state, afraid her "people" would revolt and slit her throat one night.

She was about to put the paper back when a boxed announcement caught her eye. The words seemed to leap out at her.

LADIES, COME WEST!

Brides Wanted in the Sierra. Opportunity for Fine Ladies of Daring and Adventure. Passage paid to the Gold Fields of California. Board paid for 6 mo at respectable establishment run by a Lady. Awaiting you are Gentlemen Suitors anxious for Wives in the city of Last Chance, California. Our fair city boasts a Lending Library and three Newspapers. Passage paid for your return after 6 mo if not satisfied. Only Ladies of Good Character Need Apply.

Shelby felt a tiny spurt of hope flicker inside her. She gazed out the open window to a day that seemed suddenly dazzling. Strange, she thought, that in a newspaper from the North—a place she'd been taught was filled with barbarians—she could find a way out.

Because she wouldn't have to marry anyone. It didn't say she had to marry. She'd be transported to a new land thousands of miles away. And she could be whoever she wanted out there.

A land without fathers. A land without brothers. A land without husbands. How could the West be anything less than paradise?

CHAPTER THREE
DECEPTIONS

Shelby had always had a talent for deceit. Escape turned out to be easier to arrange than she'd ever imagined.

They were paying their two-week wedding visit to Justus's aunts Lavinia and Eugenia. It was a simple matter for Shelby to pretend to still be ill. She was ordered rest by the hovering aunts. She used the time to make her plans.

While the aunts and Justus were paying a call on his many cousins, Shelby sold her wedding gift from Justus. It was a ruby necklace that had belonged to his mother.

She memorized the schedule of trains to New York and wired a Mr. Elijah Bullock to inquire about the newspaper ad. He wired back a reply to the telegraph office, telling her where the ship would be docked in New York and when it would sail. She would have to be "interviewed" beforehand, but she didn't worry about that detail.

The most difficult task turned out to be putting off

Justus every night. Shelby accomplished this with tears and fainting spells.

In only three days, she was ready.

On Thursday morning, Shelby heard the clock strike five-thirty. She glanced over to the lump on the far side of the bed. A snore whistled out through Justus's nose.

Shelby eased out of bed and padded across the floor in her bare feet. Her two small bags and a bundle of traveling clothes were downstairs, hidden in the kitchen closet.

She reached into the pocket of her dressing gown and withdrew a small purse. In addition to the money for the necklace, she had the cash her mother had secretly given her before she left home. Altogether, she'd have two hundred and fifty dollars to begin her new life.

As an afterthought, she found Justus's own leather purse and withdrew all the cash he had: fifty dollars. Why not? He would hate her enough in the morning.

She left no note, just her wedding ring and the card of the jeweler on the dresser. At least Justus would be able to buy back his mother's necklace.

Shelby cast a forlorn eye on her closet. She must be the most hard-hearted creature in the world, because in many ways, it was hardest to leave her beautiful, beautiful gowns. The peach-blossom watered silk with the pale green velvet trimming.

The shimmering emerald satin with the overskirt of clear muslin. All the bonnets, the boots, the muslins and velvets and silks.

But the gown she'd miss most of all was almost brand-new. It was made of sapphire blue velvet that matched her eyes. The tiny rosettes sewn into the lace insets of the skirt were the color of summer roses, white blushing into pink. Rose moiré ribbon threaded through the satin panels of the gored skirt.

Justus stirred, and Shelby jumped. She bundled up the cash and hurried from the room. The floorboards were cold against her bare soles.

She was halfway down the stairs when she pivoted and ran back up. She eased into the bedroom and slipped the blue velvet gown from its hanger. Bundling it under her arm, she ran lightly downstairs. It wasn't a frivolous gesture, she told herself. You never know when you might need a blue velvet gown.

She moved through the empty streets quickly, her heart pounding. She wasn't wearing stays, thanks to having no maid to lace them. It was much easier to run when your lungs didn't feel as if they were pressed against your spine.

It was a long walk to the station, and she'd never carried her own bags before. They were heavier than she'd thought. Shelby began to worry about missing the train. She had given herself thirty minutes, plenty of time, but now the blocks seemed so long!

She nearly sobbed with relief when she saw the train station ahead. Shelby checked the watch pinned to her bodice. Almost six. She'd made it.

She crossed the deserted lobby of the station and hurried to the track. Only a few people were waiting. Shelby kept well back in the shadows. She would look conspicuous, traveling alone. No Southern lady took a trip without an escort.

Shelby gasped in fright as suddenly a hand closed on her arm.

A familiar face loomed in front of her. "Do hush, Miss Shelby," Opal hissed. "They'll hear you!"

CHAPTER FOUR
In Which Our Heroine Gains a Companion

"Opal!" Shelby shrieked. "What the devil are you doing here?"

"Please hush, Mrs. Calhoun," Opal begged, looking behind her fearfully. "Somebody will hear."

Through her confusion over a slave giving her an order, Shelby felt a spurt of anger. "Don't call me that," she whispered fiercely.

There was a flicker of surprise in Opal's amber eyes at Shelby's violence. "What shall I call you then, miss?"

Shelby hesitated. "It doesn't matter now," she said finally. "I'm in a dreadful hurry, Opal, so—"

"Oh, but I think it does matter, Miss Shelby," Opal replied serenely. "Because I'm coming with you."

Shelby shook her head. "I don't know what you're thinking, Opal, but—"

"Let me tell you what I'm thinking, Miss Shelby," Opal replied in the same calm tone. "I'm thinking that you're running away from your family and Mr. Calhoun, and I aim to come along. You're going north, aren't you?"

Shelby found herself speechless. Quiet, compliant Opal, whom she *owned*, body and soul, was giving her orders!

"You're surprised that I'm here," Opal said. "But you left so many clues, Miss Shelby. And I've known you all of your life. I'm not trying to stop you. I'm trying to help you."

"W-w-why?" Shelby managed to ask.

"Because I want to go north with you," Opal answered, a trace of impatience in her voice.

Shelby tried to gather her wits. How she wished the train would come! "I don't know what you're talking about, Opal," she said coldly. "Mama is sick and I'm going home to River Glen.

"I decided to travel alone for my own reasons. And you're trying my patience. Go back to Mr. Calhoun."

Opal didn't budge. "I know you don't think that slaves have brains, Miss Shelby," she said quietly. "But even you can't rightly expect me to accept such a lie."

Shelby stamped her foot angrily. "I won't be spoken to this way!"

Opal moved closer to her. "You sold that ruby necklace Mr. Calhoun gave you. You hid your bags in the downstairs closet—I found them. I even know where you're going. The train to New York is leaving this morning."

The breath seemed to leave Shelby's body. She

was shocked at this new, strange Opal. She saw calm purpose where formerly she'd seen only deference and submission.

She heard the train whistle sound. She had no time to waste.

"What do you want?" she snapped. "Money?"

"You know yourself you shouldn't be traveling alone," Opal said. "You'll attract all manner of attention in the South without an escort. You'll be better off with your maid accompanying you."

"Opal, how can I take you?" Shelby said impatiently. "I'd be aiding and abetting a slave's escape. Do you know what could happen to me? Do you know what could happen to us?"

"I think I know better than you," Opal said drily.

"Then how can you propose such a thing?" Shelby cried. "And why should I do it?"

A faint smile played around Opal's lips. "Because you have to," she said. "You're as desperate as I am."

The whistle sounded again. Now they could hear the train clicking against the tracks as it approached the station.

"Miss Shelby, I only need to get as far as New York," Opal said quietly. "That's where my sister Ruby lives. You'll never see me again once we get there. You know I wouldn't lie, Miss Shelby."

The train moved into the station and stopped with a hiss and a squeal. Shelby heard the conductor call all aboard.

"All right," she said furiously to Opal. "I guess I haven't a choice. Just remember one thing—my name is Miss Brown, not Miss Bruneau, and *never* Miss Shelby." She had wired Mr. Bullock using the name S. Brown. She was still deciding on her new first name. It was between Sarah and Selena.

Shelby moved out from the shadows to signal the conductor. She whirled around to face Opal. "Don't say a word unless I speak to you," she hissed. "And you can start by carrying my bags!"

Shelby had always been told that Yankees were terrible creatures. Abolitionists. Federalists. Barbarians. Pushy, demanding, nosy folk with no manners who didn't know how to live with any grace at all.

But as the train sped north, Shelby's blood seemed to run faster in her veins. She seemed more . . . awake, somehow. By New Jersey, she felt reborn.

She felt her nerves flutter as they chugged into the Jersey City station at last. From here, ferries would transport the passengers to New York City.

Shelby and Opal pushed through a throng of people and found a space to stand in the lobby. Suddenly Shelby felt reluctant to see Opal go. She was saying good-bye to the last familiar face from her past.

There was no reluctance in Opal's face, however. She turned a determined gaze on Shelby. "Thank you," she said. "I won't forget what you did for me, Miss—Miss Brown," she added, flashing a lovely grin.

Shelby reached into her bag and withdrew an envelope. "I wanted to give you this, Opal. Your deed. I signed over your freedom. I had two gentlemen witness it on the train."

Opal took the papers and stared down at them.

"I don't know how legal the papers are," Shelby said, flustered. "But it's better for you to have something in case . . . well, just in case, that's all."

Keeping her head down, Opal nodded. "I appreciate it, miss."

"And good luck to you," Shelby said. She had slipped a twenty-dollar gold piece into the envelope as well. "I hope you find your sister."

"I have an address," Opal said. She looked up, clear-eyed. "I'm sure I will."

Looking around the station, Shelby wondered where Opal got her courage. A young black woman alone in a big, bustling city for the first time. Opal had never been off the Bruneau plantation except to accompany Shelby to Savannah. And here Opal was, displaying more nerve than Shelby could manage to drum up no matter how she tried.

She watched as Opal's brown homespun traveling dress and brown bonnet bobbed through the sea of people, then disappeared.

Shelby swallowed against the lump in her throat. Her stomach growled, and she realized she was hungry. There was a station restaurant next door. Did ladies eat alone in Northern restaurants? Shelby wondered. But her stomach growled again, and she decided she didn't care. A good meal might take away the empty, lost feeling in her stomach, too.

No one looked twice at her in the restaurant. Shelby ordered eggs, bacon, and coffee and almost asked for grits before she realized where she was. She would miss grits, Shelby thought hungrily. Grits and country ham and cornbread.

The eggs were greasy but plentiful, and the coffee was strong and surprisingly good. Shelby ate heartily. As she put down her coffee cup with a sigh, she decided that things were looking up.

She carried the thought with her across the lobby toward the entrance to the ferries. She consulted her telegram from Mr. Bullock, wondering which ferry would carry her closest to the New York piers.

When she looked up, she saw her father and Justus Calhoun. Their heads turned at the sight of every lady walking by. When a young woman with blond hair passed them, Justus gave a start as he peered at her. Then he shook his head.

They were looking at every face, Shelby saw. Looking for her.

CHAPTER FIVE
Miss Savannah Brown

She willed her legs not to run as she backtracked across the station toward the restaurant. She opened the door and melted inside.

She threaded through the tables, trying not to knock anything over with her wide skirt. Thank goodness she wasn't wearing her hoops.

She made for a door leading outside. Now her panic made her hurry. She actually gave a small push to one customer taking too long to count his change. His startled "Hey!" followed her out into the open air.

If she followed the building around the corner, she should see the ferries, Shelby thought frantically. Keeping her bags close to her body and her head down, she walked quickly through the crowds.

A ferry was just preparing to cast off. It was at least twenty yards from her, but Shelby didn't hesitate. She screamed at the deckhand to wait and took off.

Bags thumping, legs pumping, she dashed in a most unladylike fashion for the boat. The startled deckhand stood waiting, his hand still holding the rope. But the ferry itself was pulling away from the dock.

Six inches of gray water separated Shelby from the ferry. She met the deckhand's bright blue eyes.

"You can do it," he called. "I'll catch you. Jump!"

There was no time to think. Over the deafening blast of the horn, Shelby jumped. Her foot skidded when she hit the deck, but the sailor's hands grabbed her waist.

"You're safe," he said. He gave her waist a gentle squeeze. She almost spoke sharply to him, but she supposed he deserved a reward for catching her.

She went to the rail. White water foamed behind her as the ferry pulled away from the dock. Her father and Justus Calhoun were just walking out of the station. She saw Justus shade his eyes and look toward the ferry.

She turned her back, but it was too late. She saw Justus touch her father's arm and point.

They couldn't have recognized her, she told herself. Not from that distance. But she drew small comfort from the thought. It chilled her blood to know how quickly they had moved to find her. And how determined they were to succeed.

The hansom cab pulled away, and Shelby stood with her bags at the piers. Around her, people were bustling: passengers, freight handlers, sailors. Ahead of her was berthed the *Laconia*, the clipper ship that would carry her to a new life in California.

She walked closer, her arms aching from carrying her bags. The ship seemed deserted. Sailing was scheduled for the afternoon tide. She was early, but she'd expected to see at least one person who could help her. Someone to take her bags, give her a cabin where she could hide. What if her father and Justus found Opal? What if they were able to pick up her trail?

"Hello, *Laconia*!" she called.

No answer. Nervously, Shelby looked down the docks. What were the rules of naval etiquette, anyway? She had a right to board, didn't she?

A short, wide gangway led to the deck of the ship. Shelby strode across it, trying not to see the grayish dirty water below.

She landed on deck with a thump. She looked down and raised her skirts. The deck didn't look very clean. And the ship certainly wasn't very large. The thought of sailing across the wide deep ocean in this craft was knee-buckling.

"You're supposed to ask permission to come aboard, you know," a lazy voice said.

A rough-looking young man stood leaning against the cabin. His hair was dark and brushed his shoulders. There was reddish stubble on his cheeks, and his shirt was open at the top, exposing a strong brown neck.

One of the sailors. Shelby felt disappointed. Somehow she was expecting handsome young men smartly turned out in blue coats with brass buttons.

She gripped her bags more firmly. "I called. No one was about, so I . . ."

"Jumped aboard uninvited," the man said. His voice was low and teasing, and his eyes examined her frankly.

"I didn't get my copy of the naval rule book, I'm afraid," Shelby snapped. "Is this the usual treatment of your paying passengers?"

"Yoah *payin'* passenjas," the man mimicked gently. "I do declare, it looks like we hooked us a Southern belle."

Shelby drew herself up to her full five foot six inches. "Might I inquire as to your position on this vessel?" She gave him the same frank appraisal he had given her. "Cabin boy?"

One corner of his mobile mouth curled. "You don't talk very much like a lady, do you?" he answered, unaffected by her glare. "And I heard they want only ladies on this voyage."

"Sir, what are you suggesting?"

His eyes flicked over her black cashmere traveling cloak and dark gray muslin dress. "Your clothes seem mighty fine, is all. Why would a lady like you be taking a chance like this, going to the ends of the world?"

"That's none of your business," Shelby replied angrily. Deciding to ignore him, she picked up her bags to move to the far side of the deck. But the latch on her valise hadn't closed properly, and the bag opened, spilling some of its contents on the deck. Her blue velvet gown fell into a dirty puddle.

Before she could retrieve it, he reached for the dress with long brown fingers. "Hmm," he murmured. "Lace and velvet. A strange choice, considering the circumstances. Are you going to wear this fancy gown in the gold fields, miss?"

"Don't touch my things," Shelby snapped. She snatched the dress from his grasp and stuffed it back in her valise. She was shaking with rage. She'd never been spoken to in this manner before.

"Oh dear," the young man said. "You seem a mite ticked off. And here I thought I was making a good impression."

"You are a dirty, pest-infested hound dog," she said, pronouncing every word distinctly.

He appeared completely unconcerned by her anger. A breeze stirred his dark hair, and he kept his eyes on her speculatively. Shelby wasn't used to frank appraisals. She was used to gentlemen. She was used to young men who flattered her and were usually too bashful to even touch her hand. Timid boys had always irritated Shelby. But if this ruffian was a taste of the wide world, she should have stayed home.

"Halloo!" The voice broke into their mutual examination. "Halloo there!"

Two girls were balancing on the gangplank. The taller of the two stepped onto the deck, her russet curls swinging against her pink cheeks. She reached

over to help her companion, a slender, delicate creature with a fringe of light brown curls sticking out
from her bonnet.

The taller girl strode forward and held out her
hand. "I'm Mattie Nesbitt. You must be Elijah
Bullock. This is my sister, Ivy."

"Pleased to make your acquaintance," the man
said, reaching out and shaking Mattie's hand, then
turning his attention to Ivy. "I hope you ladies will
excuse my appearance. I was catching up on sleep
lost during the voyage, I'm afraid."

"Nonsense, Mr. Bullock," Mattie said briskly.
"We'll be traveling a long distance together. It would
be foolish to stand on ceremony."

"We are of one mind, Miss Nesbitt," he replied. He
shot Shelby a glance she thought insufferably smug.

Elijah Bullock, she thought in horror. This was
the organizer of the brides' expedition! He looked so
young, not much more than twenty, she guessed.
But he was the man who had the power to toss her
off the ship. Hadn't he said an interview was necessary before allowing her to join the expedition? And
what had she called him? she thought with a sudden
blush. *Cabin boy? Pest-infested hound dog?*

Mattie handed Elijah Bullock her letters of
introduction.

Ivy's face seemed to grow even paler as she
glanced around at the ship. "This is the vessel we'll
be sailing on to California?"

"Not the whole way, Miss Nesbitt," Eli said while he scanned the letters. "Just to Panama. From there, we travel by rail across the interior to Panama City. And then we pick up another clipper to San Francisco."

"It sounds like quite an adventure," Mattie said cheerfully. Ivy looked more dubious.

They both glanced at Shelby curiously. She realized that they were waiting for her to introduce herself. What had she decided her name should be, again?

"How do you do," she said, holding out her hand. "I'm Miss Brown."

"Ah," Elijah Bullock said. "The mysterious lady from Georgia. I received your telegram."

"I'm Mattie, and this is my sister, Ivy," Mattie said. "It seems silly not to be on a first-name basis, doesn't it?"

"What a lovely accent," Ivy said. "Where are you from, Miss Brown?"

The two questions buzzed in her head, and Shelby felt her mind go blank. *What name did I pick out, again?* She could only think of Sally, and she hated the name Sally. And where did she decide to say she was from?

"Savannah," she blurted.

Elijah looked at her curiously. "Is that where you're from, or your name?"

"My name," she said. Why not? The name was comforting, somehow. It was where she'd been most happy. "I'm from . . . Macon."

"It's a very pretty name," Ivy said.

"Unusual," Mattie observed. "Like a character's name in a book."

"Or an alias," Elijah said.

"I'm afraid I don't have any letters of introduction," Shelby said quickly. "One of my bags was stolen on the journey."

"How terrible," Ivy gasped.

"Terrible," Elijah said. But she saw the slight lift of a skeptical eyebrow.

Shelby raised her chin. Mr. Elijah Bullock probably couldn't afford to be choosy, she decided. He was most likely looking for anybody he could get. She was obviously a lady. That should be enough.

"I'd like to get settled below," she said. The sooner she got off the deck, the better. "I've had quite a long, tiring trip . . ." She pressed her fingers to her forehead for a moment. In the South, the gesture would get her an offer of a chair, a drink of water, a fan . . .

"Right," Elijah said. "Once you're below, it's the third door on your left."

Shelby opened her mouth to fire back a withering reply. But Elijah wasn't looking at her anymore. Another young woman was stepping aboard. Her fawn-colored traveling dress was modest, but obviously well tailored.

The girl nodded shyly at the group. Long eyelashes fluttered down over lovely blue-gray eyes.

Strawberry blond hair peeked out from under her bonnet. She was awfully pretty, Shelby noted with a pang. She had the kind of fragile beauty Shelby had always envied. She looked to be more angel than mortal.

Elijah moved forward quickly with a deference she'd never dreamed he could possess.

"Miss Scarborough," he said, taking her hand. "You made it after all."

"How do you do, Mr. Bullock," she said. "My friend Miss Hawkes will be arriving shortly. "She was saying good-bye to her relatives. I thought it better to come ahead."

"Of course," Elijah said. "Very considerate of you."

Shelby suppressed a snort. *And here I thought I left all the belles behind in Georgia*, she thought impatiently. Somehow it was positively galling to see another girl use the tricks that Shelby had perfected. They certainly seemed to work on Elijah Bullock.

Why hadn't Shelby thought of charming him, for pity's sake, instead of calling him names? Now this Miss Scarborough, with her expensive clothes and her fluttering eyelashes, would be receiving all the special attention. She'd get the best sleeping quarters, most likely, and her pick of the food. Shelby would be left with rancid water and hardtack.

"I think I'll go below until we sail," Shelby said, her eyes still on Elijah and the blond angel in beige.

"Are you sure it won't make you seasick, dear?" Ivy asked, concerned.

"Oh, I couldn't possibly feel any more ill than I do right now," Shelby replied sweetly.

CHAPTER SIX
TWO ARRIVALS AND A DEPARTURE

Shelby surveyed the cramped quarters below with a shocked glance. It seemed impossible that eight girls would be crammed into the narrow space.

She only had a moment to pick a top bunk and stow her luggage before her roommates arrived. For the next hour, she introduced herself and heard life stories, took compliments and gave them back, and wondered how she could possibly remember everyone's names.

First came Ivy and Mattie who shared one bunk bed. Then came a nervous girl called Henrietta and her friend Fanny who had red hair and a ringing laugh. Fanny loudly pronounced herself way too plump for her bunk. The Angel Scarborough, whose name turned out to be Jenny, took the bottom bunk opposite Shelby's, and her friend Harriet Hawkes, as plain as Jenny was pretty, took the top.

There was barely room to turn around in the cabin once all of the girls were in it. Shelby wondered irritably why a few of them didn't return to the deck, but they were all too busy getting to know each other to budge. She tucked her legs underneath her and lay back on her bunk, staring at the ceiling and wishing they'd all go away.

A shrill voice interrupted her thoughts.

"I'm sorry, I must object. I was promised the very best accommodations, and—"

Mattie poked her head out the door. "Oh dear," she murmured. "Trouble."

"What is it?" Ivy asked.

"It's that Narcissa Pratt," Mattie whispered. She listened for a moment, then poked her head back in the cabin. "Apparently there's a . . . well, a woman of color on board, and Narcissa won't room with her."

"Miss Nesbitt?" Elijah's voice came to them clearly. "Could I speak with you a moment?"

Mattie slipped out of the cabin. In a moment, she was back, her face flushed but her manner composed. "I trust there would be no objection if the newest arrival slept in our cabin. We have plenty of room."

Her bright blue eyes dared one person in the jammed cabin to refuse. No one did. Shelby imagined that no one would even think of it.

Mattie nodded firmly. "All right, Mr. Bullock," she called.

Eli walked in with Opal Pollard. Shelby sat up, bumping her head on the bulkhead. Opal saw her and Shelby gave a quick negative shake of her head. Opal's gaze moved smoothly away.

"You can sleep here, Miss Pollard," Elijah said. "And I apologize for . . . any inconvenience." He turned to the rest of the girls. "We're getting under way, ladies. You might want to come up on deck."

Shelby slowly trailed after the girls. She was dying to confront Opal, but the girl eluded her, slipping off and joining a group of passengers in the stern.

Up on deck, the sailors were moving, untying lines and calling orders. Most of the girls crowded against the railing for a better view, but Shelby preferred to stay in the back. She didn't want to be visible from shore.

She forgot about Opal as she listened to the cries of the sailors, the orders given and repeated. Her heart lifted. The gulls wheeled overhead and the faint rays of the sun cast a feeble glow on the water. She couldn't wait for the ship to pull away from the dock.

Down the pier, a slight figure ran, waving one slender arm. Behind her, two sailors, each carrying a trunk, struggled to keep up. As the girl approached the ship, Shelby could just make out her words.

"Blast and damn! Don't you dare leave without me!"

The girl's bonnet flew off her head and flopped down her back, held by its ribbons around her neck. Curly dark hair spilled from its pins and streamed down her shoulders.

The sailor who had been bringing in the gangplank quickly lowered it again. The girl raised her skirts and hopped onto it with the ease of a dancer. She motioned at the two men behind her to hurry as she landed with a soft thump on the deck.

The men threw the trunks to the waiting sailors. The girl caught the sailors staring at her legs and hesitated a few moments before dropping her skirts. She smiled a decidedly wicked smile at the cutest sailor.

Definitely not a lady, Shelby thought.

Unconcerned at the stares of the passengers, the girl blew away a stray curl from her eye, untied her straggling bonnet, and smoothed the skirt of what Shelby felt was a rather garish striped silk dress. The ship blasted its horn and began to move out of the berth.

"Made it," she called to Shelby. "In the nick, I'd say."

She stepped up to the railing. The buildings of Manhattan began to recede as the ship sailed away into the harbor.

"Glad to see the blasted back of that city," she said pleasantly. She turned to Shelby and held out a hand. Startling emerald eyes twinkled in a delicate, pretty face. "I'm Eden."

"Savannah," Shelby answered. She felt the deck move beneath her feet as the clipper picked up speed. The sound of the horn made her jump.

Savannah, she thought, as she and Eden both turned without a word and looked out to the open sea. From now on she would train herself to call herself by that name, even in her head.

She liked the sound of it. It was a name for a girl who didn't simper at someone just because they wore pants. Who wasn't polite if it didn't suit. Who didn't waste her time with foolishness. A new name for a new life. She couldn't wait to begin it.

CHAPTER SEVEN
SALTING THE MINE

They were blessed with good weather until they reached the coast of Florida, when heavy swells set in. Most of the brides headed for the upper deck, gulping air in an attempt to relieve their queasy stomachs.

Savannah spotted a familiar form darting toward the stern. At last, Opal was alone. By sticking to Mattie and Ivy or one of the other girls, she'd managed to avoid Savannah for days now.

Opal stood with a death grip on the railing. "At last," Savannah said, grasping her elbow. Opal jumped, then moaned. "Miss Shelby, please don't rattle me like that. I'm doing my best at the moment to keep down what feels like every morsel I ever ate in my life."

"It's Savannah, not Miss Shelby, and why did you follow me aboard ship? Tell me or I'll throw you overboard, you worthless, no-account . . ."

"All right, Miss Savannah," Opal pleaded. "Just don't—shake me again. I'm not following you. I left you in the station at Jersey City."

"Did you see anyone?" Savannah asked anxiously.

"Lots of folk," Opal said, puzzled. Then light dawned in her eyes. "You mean someone from home? Did you?"

"Never mind," Savannah said. "Just go on."

"I went to Ruby's last address, but she wasn't there. The woman living there told me she'd signed on as a washerwoman on a clipper ship going to San Francisco. Well, I didn't know what to do—not knowing one living soul in New York City. Then I remembered the advertisement I found in your valise. I decided it was worth a try to get free passage west."

"You mean you knew where I was headed that whole time?" Savannah demanded.

Opal closed her eyes as the ship dipped into the trough of a swell. "It wasn't hard to figure out. So I came to the pier. Mr. Bullock is a good man. Said it didn't matter about my color. I think it could all work out, Miss Shel—"

"If I hear you call me Shelby again, so help me I'll keelhaul you with my own two hands, Opal Pollard," Savannah said fiercely.

"I don't know what keelhauling is, but I'm sure it can't be much worse than what I'm feeling right now," Opal moaned. "But I swear."

"And remember, don't let on you know me," Savannah added. "I don't want anybody knowing how I came to be here."

"You might imagine that I'm not that anxious to confide my life story, either," Opal said.

Savannah looked at the girl, trying to hide her surprise. Opal was speaking to her in a new way. She was a free woman, of course—Savannah had freed her. But somehow Savannah hadn't figured on Opal *acting* free, as well as being free. It was very disconcerting.

"Now, if you'll excuse me, Miss Shelby . . ." Opal said.

And now she was *dismissing* her!

"Not Shelby!" she hissed. "Savannah!"

But Opal only turned away. She hung over the railing and retched into the sea.

Savannah turned away quickly. Her own stomach was beginning to lurch. To her surprise, she looked straight into the shrewd green eyes of Eden Moran, who was standing only a few feet away.

Did she hear me? Savannah wondered nervously. But Eden merely waved as she continued her walk on the pitching deck.

Savannah tried to shake off an uneasy feeling. It didn't really matter if Eden had heard her. The girl was harmless. And she was way too tiny to be much of a threat to anybody.

Elijah Bullock hated the sea. He did not like to feel the deck shifting under his feet. He felt more secure tunneling into rock than he did on top of the moving ocean. At least ten times a day he had to stop himself from imagining what it must be like to drown.

Eli lit a thin cigar, praying it wouldn't make him seasick. He wished he had someone to talk to, but he wasn't tempted to join the girls. It was best to keep himself aloof from fifteen man-hungry women.

Keeping himself aloof just might be the toughest part of his assignment, especially when it came to Jenny Scarborough. Now there was a lovely sight, with her sad gray eyes and that silky hair the color of apricots. She was definitely the beauty of the group, no matter what Savannah Brown thought, with her airs and graces and her tossing of that wild blond mane.

Eli sighed. He had been distracted and busy that first day, and had never gotten a chance to ask Savannah the right questions. He had the feeling the girl was running from something. Most of the brides had accepted his offer out of sheer poverty, like the Nesbitt girls. Or like Jenny, whose well-born parents had died and left her penniless.

He had to be careful. His father had warned him, his brother had warned him, even his mother, with the most profound delicacy, had warned him. Invitations such as this invited bad women. The adventuress would see an opportunity. The girl of easy virtue would see a way to make her fortune. The girls had to have references, his mother had insisted. If he brought home the wrong sort to Last Chance, his father would never let him have responsibility again. And he had only just agreed this year to let Eli and Josiah take over the running of the mine.

They were young for the job, but they were eager. It had taken them months, but they had won the men's respect. The only thing they hadn't been able to do was get the miners to stay put. They were constantly dealing with work shortages.

Because the trouble with miners was that they'd pack up in a minute if they heard about a strike in Oregon or Colorado. But what better way to get men to settle down than to import pretty women to tempt them? Miners were used to coarser girls, girls with bad teeth and raucous laughs, girls you had to pay to spend time with. Young women like these would be worth staying in town for. They were the marrying kind.

A shrill scream made him jump. Eli threw his cheroot in the sea and took off after the sound. Had one of those fool girls fallen overboard?

He ran toward the bow, desperately clutching the rail when the ship lurched and settled in the next wave.

But it was only Henrietta Burdine again. She was afraid of sharks, sailors, and pirates. Apparently she'd added a moderately rough sea to the list.

"Oh, Mr. Bullock," Henrietta said. "I'm so glad you're here. If I wasn't already completely distracted by this terrible sea, now I'd have been scared out of my wits. One of the passengers was talking to us of California. He was there for the forty-nine rush. He said there are towns called Garrote and Hangtown and . . ."

"Gouge Eye," Eden supplied, grinning.

"He said there's murderers 'round every bush," Henrietta said in a trembling voice.

Silently, Eli cursed the ship's male passengers. They were all enjoying teasing the brides a little too enthusiastically.

"Now, Miss Burdine," he said in a soothing tone. "That might have been true at one time. California is a young land. But we're a state now, with laws and courts and jails. There's no Hangtown any-more—it's called Placerville now. Last Chance is as close to civilized as you can get this side of Boston."

"Tell us about it, Mr. Bullock," Mattie urged.

Eli saw the brides draw closer. "Well, now," he said. "It's the most beautiful land you've ever seen. We're cradled in what's called the foothills of the Sierra. But don't think of Eastern hills. They're like . . . like anthills compared to what we have out west. And our valleys aren't just valleys—they're canyons. I can take you to places on the American River with walls so steep around you, you could barely walk a mule downstream."

He had them now. Their eyes were on him, their faces interested, open. Only Eden Moran was watching him with a slightly mocking air. He saw

Savannah approaching, and he raised his voice to tempt her closer.

"And the weather—well, it's close to perfect. The sun shines seven days out of ten. The summer rain is gentle and fragrant, and it only comes late in the afternoon if at all. And the snow is so soft and pretty you think of clouds, not frost."

"Oh, my," Henrietta breathed.

"It sounds so lovely," Ivy said.

"That's when we'll be arriving. You're going to see trees so tall they scrape the bluest sky this side of heaven." Eli continued, "Sweet green meadows softer than a featherbed. Rivers so clear and deep you can count the fish swimming at the bottom. But there's no need for a rod—the salmon and trout jump right up into your hands. The gentle mountains cradle the valleys like a mother with her newborn babe."

Eli's gaze swept them. He had them all in the palm of his hand, he thought. Even Savannah Brown was listening, though she was pretending not to. "And there's veins of gold running through it all," he finished. "It's God's country, pure and simple."

"Tell us more," Fanny Mulrooney urged.

"Tell us about the miners," Adele Dumont said with a saucy smile, and the girls giggled.

Eden withdrew to the railing. Savannah saw her smile, and she drifted over to stand next to her.

"Why are you laughing?" she murmured.

"I have a feeling our Mr. Bullock is salting the mine a bit," Eden said.

"Salting the mine?"

Eden grinned. "It's a confidence game. You scatter nuggets around in a played-out mine entrance to convince someone to take it off your hands. It's in Mr. Bullock's best interest to describe a mining town as paradise."

"You don't think he is telling the truth?" Savannah asked. She looked over at Eli again. He happened to look up at that instant, just as the sun appeared from behind a cloud. It lit his face, and she realized with a shock that in the right light, one could almost consider him handsome. His eyes were the clearest blue she'd ever seen, the color of sunlight through water.

The tiniest of thrills tiptoed up her spine, making her shiver despite the heat. She realized that since they'd been at sea, even if she was walking alone or reading or just staring out to sea, she had always been aware of where he was.

Eden glanced at her, amused, and Savannah tore her gaze away. "I wouldn't call him handsome," Eden remarked.

"Oh no," Savannah said carelessly. "His nose is too big."

Across the deck, Eli tried to pay attention to Fanny's joking questions. The look he'd just received from Savannah's dark blue eyes had somehow rocked him. Or maybe it was just the pitching sea. He hoped so.

Because the girl bothered him. She had the clothes and the manner of a lady, but such things can be bought and learned. Something just didn't fit. Behind that dripping molasses accent and those deep blue eyes, she was hiding secrets.

Looking around at the faces surrounding him, Eli made a decision. Out of all of them, the scared ones, the bold ones, the happy ones, the sad ones— even the brassy Eden Moran—he was going to keep his eye on Miss Savannah Brown.

CHAPTER EIGHT
SOMEWHERE OFF THE COAST OF PANAMA

"*Cholera!*" Henrietta Burdine cried. Her thin nose twitched in alarm. Ever since leaving their last American port of New Orleans, Henrietta had grown more and more anxious.

"I apologize ma'am." The male passenger bowed politely. "I didn't mean to give you the impression that cholera was going to carry you off in Panama."

"Oh, thank heavens," Henrietta said. She fanned herself vigorously with her hand, which only served to make her hotter than before.

"Why you could just as soon be taken by the yellow fever or malaria," the man concluded.

With a sigh, Henrietta swooned against Ivy's shoulder. Ivy fanned her and shot the man a scornful look.

"Don't worry, Hen," Eden said soothingly. "We'll all chip in and buy you the prettiest little coffin."

Henrietta burst into tears. Eden winked at Savannah, who looked away. There was something insinuating about the girl's behavior toward her that made her uneasy.

"Now, miss, settle down," the man said, looking unsettled at Henrietta's wails. "I'm sure you'll make it safely to California. One thing for sure, you'll see the elephant."

"Elephants, too?" Hen squeaked. "Oh, my—"

They hadn't noticed when Eli had joined them, but now he stood at the edge of the group. He gave the man an icy glance. Though Eli was at least ten years younger and twenty pounds lighter, the man bowed and moved off.

Eli turned to the girls. "It's just an expression, ladies," he said. "It means you're on a great journey and will see new wonders. And you will change, too—maybe in ways you'd never have dreamed."

Savannah felt Eli's eyes on her. She swept a stray wisp of hair away from her eyes impatiently. Why was he always *looking* at her? Between his looks and Eden's winks, she was inclined to jump off at the next port. Even if it was in cholera-ridden Panama.

She walked ahead of the other girls to get away from him. But in a moment, he was by her side.

"Lovely weather," Eli said.

"If you like humidity," Savannah said.

"I'm glad the rough seas are behind us," Eli remarked. "And my stomach is grateful."

Savannah tossed her head. "I wasn't sick for a moment."

"I'm glad to have a chance to chat," Eli went on.

"Perhaps I can learn something about the mysterious Miss Brown."

"Mysterious, Mr. Bullock?" she asked. She tried to walk faster, but with his long legs he kept pace with her easily.

"I've seen you walking alone," Eli said. "The other girls stick together, talking of families and what they've left behind. But you never do."

"Just because I'm not a sentimental ninny like the other girls doesn't render me mysterious, Mr. Bullock," Savannah countered.

"Maybe not mysterious," he said. "Maybe *intriguing* is a better word?"

Savannah looked out over the turquoise sea. "Hardly intriguing. I'd say I was close to downright tedious, Mr. Bullock."

"I doubt that very much," Eli said smoothly. "By the way, did you know Miss Moran before the voyage?"

Savannah's heart thumped uneasily. "No, I've only just met her."

"Funny," he said. "You seem to be rather intimate for such a short acquaintance."

"Perhaps I make friends easily," Savannah remarked. "I'm friendly with all the brides."

"I'm sure you are," Eli murmured. "With the . . . sentimental ninnies, as you called them?" Before Savannah could respond, he bowed. "I should allow you to return to your good friends."

The irony that dripped from his words gave

Savannah the itch to push him overboard. From now on, she decided, her first order of business was to steer clear of Elijah Bullock.

It was after midnight on a hot night so still she could hear the plash of a fish breaking the surface. The sounds of the other girls' quiet breathing told Savannah that they were asleep.

How could they sleep in all this heat? Savannah wondered, irritably kicking off the damp sheet. What she needed was a breath of air.

Slipping out of her bunk, she slid her bare feet into her shoes and wiggled into her lightest dress of white pique. She didn't bother with petticoats. She doubted she'd meet anyone topside this late at night.

She eased out of the cabin and tiptoed up the stairs to the deck. The night air was sweltering and not much fresher than the air below. She took a deep breath of it anyway.

"I see we had the same idea," a soft voice said.

Savannah turned. She hadn't even seen Eden in the darkness. She was stretched out on one of the deck chairs, looking straight up at the night sky. If Savannah had been worried about going on deck without her petticoat, Eden put her fears to rest. The girl was clad only in her nightgown and a filmy silk shawl.

Lazily, Eden waved at the chair next to her. "Sit down, Miss Brown. It's a darn sight better up here than listening to Narcissa snore."

Savannah perched on the edge of the chair. "I just came up for a minute," she said.

"You can't sleep in the heat, either," Eden said, fanning herself lazily. "We must be two of a kind."

Savannah straightened. "I hardly think so, Miss Moran."

Eden ignored Savannah's frosty tone. "But I'm so fascinated by you, Savannah," she drawled. "Maybe it's my fascination with your home state. They say we might have a war between North and South; can you believe such a thing?"

"No," Savannah said.

"Which reminds me of a strange experience I had on the pier before we sailed," Eden said. "I was running to catch the ship—"

"Yes," Savannah said. "We all remember your arrival vividly. Especially the sailors."

"—and I bumped into—I mean, literally bumped into—two gentlemen on the docks."

"I have a feeling that encountering strange gentlemen is a frequent occurrence in your life, Miss Moran," Savannah said.

"Occasionally," Eden said cheerfully. "But my point, if I can seem to locate it in all this heat, was— oh yes. The men were *Southern*."

Despite the humid night, Savannah felt a chill. "Oh?" she said carefully.

"Yes, you don't meet many Southerners in New

York these days, considering the political situation," Eden went on. "One was older, a little stout, but a fine-looking figure of a man. And the other was young and *very* well-dressed. They were looking for a lady. A young lady of seventeen. Name of Shelby Bruneau Calhoun. They asked me to keep an eye out for her. Said there was a reward. I have their address. . . ."

"Rather difficult for you to keep an eye out, isn't it?" Savannah tried to speak lightly. "Being that you're halfway round the world now?"

"Not as difficult as you might imagine," Eden said, looking out over the dark sea. "Did you know I speak a little French? My dear daddy taught me. He's an Irish lord, but he traveled quite widely."

An Irish lord, my foot, Savannah thought angrily. Only a blackguard would have bred this vixen of a daughter.

"Did you know that *brun eau* means brown water?" Eden said. "Not a very pretty name in English, is it? I would shorten it, wouldn't you? If I wanted to change it, I mean."

Savannah jackknifed to her feet. "It's so late. I should get below."

Eden stood and put a hand on her arm. "Now, don't get all flustered; it's way too hot. I'm not going to tell on you, Shelby Savannah Bruneau Brown. I figure a girl's got her own reasons for running away from a situation. I just wanted to let you know that I knew, that's all."

"That's all?" Savannah asked in disbelief.

"For now," Eden replied serenely.

"I knew it," Savannah said furiously. "What do you want, Eden?"

"It's funny, I can't think of a thing at the moment," Eden said lightly. "But I might one day. And it just warms my heart to think I'll be able to call on you."

"This is blackmail," Savannah spit out.

"Oh, dear, what a nasty word," Eden said, her lips drawing together in a tiny pout. "I'd rather call it a very significant *friendship*. Wouldn't you?"

CHAPTER NINE
SEEING THE ELEPHANT

From his position behind a post, Eli saw Eden move away from Savannah. Slender legs flashed through the filmy material as she made her languid way below.

Savannah turned back to the railing. She clutched it and looked out to sea. Although her back was to Eli, he could see the tense way she held herself. She was furious.

What's going on with those two? he wondered. The ship wasn't large, and it was shrinking by the day. He knew everyone aboard now. And he knew that little Eden, with her dimples and her sweet smile, had already cleaned out most of the men on board with nightly poker games.

Secret meetings at midnight. Angry words. Savannah must be an accomplice of some sort, Eli thought worriedly. That was all he needed, to bring two sweet-faced confidence women to Last Chance.

His town had its share of poker games. But

they were friendly games, played for reasonable stakes. Professional gamblers were politely but firmly escorted to the town limits. He wasn't about to march two of them right up Main Street and pay for their board!

He'd be the laughingstock of Last Chance. And when you're twenty-three years old and running the biggest moneymaking business in town, you can't afford to make those kinds of mistakes.

Eli walked toward Savannah Brown. He had to find out, once and for all, what kind of woman she was. He needed to bait the hook.

She heard his footsteps and turned just as he came up. *What an actress,* he thought admiringly. There was no trace of anger on her face. Just natural surprise.

"Mr. Bullock! So you're having trouble sleeping in this weather as well."

"Yes. It's hot," Eli said rather unimaginatively. But he was diverted by the sight of Savannah's throat, bared to the night air. She had unbuttoned her white dress, and he could see the sheen of perspiration on her skin. Her blond hair was loose and flowed down her back.

She turned back to the railing. "We dock in Panama tomorrow. Eden has scared Henrietta half to death with tales of natives stripping down to . . . well, the bare necessities to pilot boats down the Chagres River."

Eli smiled. "That might have been true at one time. But we'll be taking a train across the interior."

"Hen will be relieved to hear it," Savannah remarked. "But I have a suspicion that Narcissa will be disappointed."

Eli laughed, and she joined in. It was the first easy moment that had ever been between them.

"The overland voyage used to be dangerous," Eli said. "Cholera and malaria struck many down. There's quite a large American cemetery in Panama City. It's much safer now. Only six or seven weeks to California. It took my family six months to go around the Horn ten years ago."

"So you were early settlers in California," Savannah said.

"Yes, we were there before the rush. My father started a ranch near Sacramento. It did fairly well. We had managed to make some money when gold was discovered at Sutter's Mill. Pa went right out and bought a prospecting pan."

"And he got lucky," Savannah said.

"And he got lucky," Eli agreed. "I was only eleven at the time, but we worked the stream, my brother and me, right beside him. You had to worry about claim jumpers. We were never far from our rifles in those days. We do placer mining now—blasting right into the rock."

Savannah watched his face. He had drifted back to the past. She thought of her brother Cole at eleven, with his pampered hands. And she pictured a slender, younger Eli, bending over an icy stream for hours to pan for gold.

She didn't know how they'd drifted into an ordinary, pleasant conversation. But she'd keep it going. Maybe the way to divert Eli Bullock was to charm him. She could be a nice person like Jenny Scarborough if she really tried.

"The early days were wild," Eli said reflectively. "We saw men shoot each other over a barrel of flour. One fellow set up a business in Last Chance—ten dollars for a look at a lady's bonnet and boots. He made his fare back home to Illinois."

"Oh, my," Savannah said lightly. "I hope you're not planning to sell off the brides."

"We're a bit more genteel now," Eli said. "Last Chance was a rip-roaring town at one time. But we've managed to civilize it."

"Ah," Savannah said. "That's why you need us ladies. For our civilizing influence."

"Ladies do have a tendency to . . . gentle up a town, you might say," Eli said. He turned and leaned against the rail to face her. "It's all that softness and smoothness, you know."

Savannah's throat suddenly felt tight. Eli's gaze had changed. The amusement had left his eyes. He looked absolutely intent on her.

He reached out and trailed one finger down the inside of her forearm. "Like that," he said.

She swallowed. What was happening? Why was Eli suddenly acting like a suitor, not an enemy?

His fingers wrapped around her wrist. He must be able to feel her pulse racing. She willed it to slow, but her heart only beat faster.

She'd kissed a few boys back home. She'd let them hold her hand. And Justus—well, he'd embraced her once, before she'd pretended to feel faint. She'd felt his body, hard against hers, for just one moment. It had been a glimpse into married life that had frightened her.

But this was different. She *wanted* this. She wanted him to touch her just that way, with his fingers lightly stroking her skin.

It was a night of the new moon, and the darkness felt thick and heavy. She could see Eli's eyes, those strange, light eyes, and they seemed to hold her, trap her, and she was drifting, borne along by a powerful current.

He pulled her against him. She bumped against his chest and felt his heartbeat underneath her fingers. So his pulse was racing, too.

His gaze was almost puzzled as he bent his head. She closed her eyes as she felt his kiss. It was soft, searching. A strange liquidity ran through her legs. When his tongue teased her lip, her mouth opened. She was surprised, embarrassed, when his tongue slid inside her mouth. But apparently this was the way kissing was done in California. No wonder—it was quite . . . wonderful.

With one part of his brain, Eli noted Savannah's response. The girl was no innocent. But if he had started this just to test the waters, now he was drowning in her.

His hands roamed over her body, the skin of her throat, her breasts. He felt her moan, and he knew she was at the edge of her control, too. He smelled her scent, the perfume rising from her breasts, and it roared through his body like a runaway train.

Eli whirled her around and pressed her down on the deck chair. Now his body covered hers completely. He slid his knee in between her legs and felt her shudder. She clutched him against her. Her lips against his neck felt warm and greedy.

He ran his tongue along her throat, down to where her breasts began to swell. *I was right. She's not a lady.*

Eli froze. What was he doing? If he was right, he couldn't encourage her. He couldn't become involved with a girl like this. He was wrong to take advantage of her, no matter if she was taking advantage of him.

Where he came from, there were only two kinds of women. One kind lived in the pink-shuttered house that he was forbidden to visit. The other kept their eyes lowered and blushed if he cursed by accident. Savannah seemed to fall into neither category, and that confused him.

"Eli?"

She rose, her indigo eyes cloudy, her hair mussed. He had unbuttoned most of her bodice, and he saw a creamy breast nudge against the lace of her camisole. He groaned.

"Button your dress," he said gruffly, turning away.

Savannah looked down at herself. Her nakedness came as a shock. She had lost all notion of where she was. *He really is a gentleman,* she thought. He stopped when she could not.

She put a hand on his back and felt the heat of his skin through his shirt.

"We'd better get below," he said.

Without another word, he walked her to her cabin. She was too shy to look at him and quickly slipped inside.

She stood against the closed door for a moment. She ran her hands over bare skin still tingling where Eli had touched her. For the first time in her life, she felt she understood everything. Marriage. Courting. Her cousin Winnie's blushes whenever her new husband walked into the room.

All of it, all that heated blood and those wild kisses, had been going on underneath her very own nose. Savannah wanted to laugh out loud.

Mattie lifted her head sleepily. She yawned. "What's going on?"

Savannah tiptoed between the bunks. "Don't look now," she whispered. "But I think I just saw the elephant."

CHAPTER TEN
THREE RUDE AWAKENINGS

A hand shook her shoulder, but Savannah ignored it. She was in the middle of the most wonderful dream.

"Wake up, Savannah!" a voice scolded. "It's bath day, remember?"

She burrowed into her pillow with a groan. Bath day meant the girls had to rise with the sun. Even though Narcissa supervised the hanging of blankets on deck so that not a crack showed, minister's daughter Harriet insisted on doing it at dawn, just in case.

Savannah yawned in Mattie's wide-awake face. "All right," she grumbled. Mattie grinned and tossed her a towel.

Savannah climbed topside, wincing at the bright sun. The glare promised a day as hot as yesterday. She stripped to her camisole and pantalettes and began to wash. If only she could have privacy to think about the night before! But that was the trouble with being aboard ship. Just when you needed a bathtub with plenty of hot water, you got stuck with a sponge and Fanny Mulrooney.

Savannah felt in the midst of a pleasurable suspense. This morning she found herself pondering a suddenly delicious question: *When will I see him again?* There wasn't much mystery to the answer. She was stuck on a steamboat after all. But it was odd how much fun it was to speculate.

She dreamily dipped the sponge in water and watched it trail down her arm. She thought of Eli's kisses and sighed. She barely heard the murmur of Fanny's voice, going on and on like the ceaseless murmur of the waves.

Fanny had finished her own bath and was combing her unruly red hair. If she mailed a letter in Panama, would her sister Sarah receive it? Poor Sarah had been so brokenhearted at her going. So convinced Fanny would come to a terrible end.

Then Savannah gave a start at the sound of Eli's name.

"I'm sure Mr. Bullock will be mailing a letter in Panama City," Fanny mused. "He'll take the first opportunity to write his sweetheart, most likely."

Savannah dropped the sponge in the bucket. "His what?"

"His sweetheart," Fanny said. "Didn't you know he was engaged? You're always walking off by yourself, Savannah; you miss all the news. It's too bad, isn't it? I thought for sure he had eyes for Jenny. Now, maybe I should wait until San Francisco to write. But Sarah will be worrying about me, I'm sure. She's only fifteen—"

Savannah retrieved the sponge. She squeezed it hard, and the water ran out. *Engaged.* And he had kissed her like that? No honorable person would have done such a thing. She pushed aside the nagging thought that no honorable young woman would have let a young man lie on top of her on a deserted deck.

Suddenly the speculation over how he would act when he saw her next wasn't pleasurable at all.

"Good morning, Miss Brown."

"Good morning, Mr. Bullock."

"Miss Brown. I—I wanted to say . . ."

"Yes, Mr. Bullock?"

"That I regret . . ."

"Yes, Mr. Bullock?"

"My shameful behavior . . ."

Savannah kept her parasol tilted to shade her face. She felt an overwhelming devastation sweep over her. It had just been the heat, the night, the sense of being alone in the middle of a vast ocean. Or had it been something far more basic, what her mother had always whispered about a man's "depraved" nature?

Savannah felt puzzled. If that was true, she was depraved, too, wasn't she?

She'd have to think on it. But until then, she had her pride.

"Let's say no more about it, Mr. Bullock," she said.

"I take full responsibility," Eli said, struggling to make it through this awkward, agonizing conversation. "It was—"

She laid a hand on his arm to stop him. "Mr. Bullock, you are an engaged man. I can only guess at your feelings of utter degradation today."

Eli's mouth closed with a snap.

She dropped her hand. She gestured toward the Panamanian shoreline. "But here we are on the other side of the world. How would your betrothed ever possibly discover your . . . shameful behavior?"

Eli pondered this. Was she threatening him—or reassuring him? Her serene gaze told him nothing.

Savannah looked down, fluttering her eyelashes, and spoke in a low, trembling voice. "Mr. Bullock. Whatever . . . *horror* you may feel as to your *vile* and *base* conduct"—Savannah paused delicately— "well, that should be punishment enough."

She swept off, looking the picture of innocence in white pique. How had she managed to make him feel even more of a worm than he was? Eli struggled mightily to restrain himself. It just wouldn't look right for the leader of the expedition to dash his brains out against the cabin wall.

Panama was a blur of heat, humidity, and green jungle. During the railway journey, Henrietta complained of soot, hunger, thirst, and fatigue, and got six cinders in her eye. The hotel in Panama City had bedbugs. Their connecting clipper had left without them. Eli had to bribe the captain of another ship to take them on. Savannah hadn't seen such a display of masculine anger since her father caught her reading *Uncle Tom's Cabin*. She enjoyed every minute of it.

But the sailing to San Francisco went without incident. There were breathtaking views of Mexican jungles and golden California hills. Their luck held when Henrietta caught a cold and kept to her bunk for three entire days.

And through every mile they sailed along the California coastline, Eli Bullock never spoke to Savannah Brown directly again.

They barely had time to register the breathtaking bay of San Francisco before Eli shepherded them aboard a small steamship, which carried them up the river to Sacramento. There they were met by Willie Joe, a black man with a handsome smile who was too shy to look any of them in the eye and appeared rooted to the spot at the sight of Opal.

He drove one wagon, Eli drove the other, and the girls bumped over a road that started out quite sedately, but ended up clinging to a mountain.

Savannah resolutely kept her eyes ahead and wished Henrietta would do the same. Every time she sneaked a peek at the thousand-foot drop, she shrieked with alarm. The cries gradually turned into a constant, high-pitched hum of panic. It didn't stop until Fanny blindfolded her with her hanky.

They had barely recovered from the ride when the wagons creaked into Last Chance. The brides huddled in the wagons, staring out with disbelieving eyes.

"This is . . . it?" Henrietta asked.

"I'm sure not," Ivy murmured.

"This is the *town*?" Fanny blurted.

"Mon dieu," Adele Dumont breathed.

It was now late afternoon, and the sun slanted low through the pines. Through the gathering dusk they saw rough wooden planks thrown down across what looked like a river of mud. The buildings seemed to be a collection of shacks with alarmingly sagging roofs. In places the mud was dotted with garbage, empty tins, bottles, a pair of red suspenders. Through the gloom, Savannah thought she glimpsed a dead mule.

"This isn't a town," she announced. "It's a swamp."

CHAPTER ELEVEN
In Which the Brides Meet Their Landlady

It began to rain. They sat, silent and numb, as the wagons slowly creaked down Main Street.

"Things do tend to look disagreeable when you arrive in the evening," Ivy said finally.

"We didn't expect paradise, did we?" Mattie tried. But no one replied.

"Paradise it isn't," Eden said cheerfully. "Savannah is right. It's the biggest mudhole I've ever seen."

"Now there's a fine house," Mattie said.

They passed a trim brick house with pink shutters and a red door. Unlike the other buildings, this one had a freshly swept walk in front. There were even flowers planted in the side plot of land.

"That's the boarding house, I'll warrant," Ivy said. "Didn't Mr. Bullock tell us that we'd be lodged in the finest place in town?"

A woman appeared at the upper window. She placed a candle on the sill and caught sight of the two wagons. She leaned forward to get a better look, her dark hair spilling over what Savannah suddenly realized was a very indecent wrapper.

"That must be Annie Friend," Henrietta said, squinting nearsightedly.

Eden laughed. "I surely hope not."

Just then a man approached the house and walked in the front door without knocking. For an instant, they heard the sound of light laughter.

"Seems like a gay place," Fanny said.

Eden laughed again. "Don't you girls have eyes in your head? It's a cathouse."

"A what?" Henrietta asked.

"Oh, for heaven's sake. The place where soiled doves come to roost," she added mockingly.

Henrietta gasped. "That was a bad woman?"

"I'm getting on the next stage out of here," Harriet said, her voice wobbling. "I'm a minister's daughter."

"What do you expect from a mining town, you ninnies?" Eden asked carelessly. Her eyes raked the street ahead.

Probably looking for the saloon, Savannah thought disdainfully. She'd managed to steer clear of Eden for the remainder of the voyage, and she fully intended to keep doing so.

Eli turned off the main street. He and Willie Joe stopped their wagons in front of a brick house that looked the same as every other dingy place they'd passed, only worse.

The girls silently jumped down from the wagons. Eli and Willie Joe busily began to pile the luggage on the rough wooden porch. Then Eli strode to the door, which consisted of four planks nailed together. The doorknob was a piece of twine wrapped around a stick. Eli gave one blow to the door with his fist.

"Ah," Savannah murmured. "The frontier version of a polite knock, I assume."

"Annie!" Eli hollered. "We're here!" He shouldered open the door.

The girls followed hesitantly. There was just enough light coming from the streaked windows for them to make out a dingy hallway. Behind her, Savannah heard a gasp.

"Raise your skirts," Mattie whispered.

She looked down. Now that her eyes were accustomed to the dim light, she saw that the floor was stained with tobacco juice. It had even pooled in various sunken areas of the floor.

A steep narrow staircase disappeared in the gloom. One rickety table stood illuminated by a gas lamp. It was piled with guns.

"Annie doesn't like guns in her house," Eli explained. "You have to leave them at the door if you want to play."

"Play?" Eden asked hopefully. "You mean cards?"

But Eli didn't get a chance to answer.

A door at the end of the hallway banged open and a woman stepped through it. At least it *seemed* to be a woman, by the look of the soft mounds underneath her plaid flannel shirt. She was dressed in trousers and boots, and she strode toward Eli, a smile on her broad, weathered face.

"Well, as I live and breathe. I thought you were dead, Eli Bullock!" she chortled.

"What are you talking about, Annie? I'm only a week late," Eli protested, dusting the mud off his pants with his hat.

"If a man goes missing for more'n a month round here, I get to figurin' he's dead," Annie replied cheerfully. "And by gum, I'm usually right!"

"This is our chaperon?" Narcissa whispered.

Annie peered at Eli in the gloom. "And you don't look much the worse for wear, either. Still the handsomest varmint in the Sierra Nevada."

"Then I think we are in trouble, girls," Savannah muttered. Eden laughed.

"Are these them?" Annie boomed, pointing to the girls.

"*This* is our chaperon, Mr. Bullock?" Harriet Hawke asked tremulously. "I'm a minister's daughter, sir. You promised me lodgings in a respectable house."

"Now, wait a second—," Annie started.

"It's dirty," Henrietta wailed.

"We mean no disrespect, ma'am," Ivy said to Annie Friend. "But we were led to believe that we'd be lodged in a lady's boardinghouse, and, if you'll excuse me for saying so, this appears to be a . . . well, a . . . ."

"Flophouse for miners?" Annie supplied helpfully.

Ivy looked faint. "Precisely. Thank you."

Annie scratched her head. "Well, I guess I *did* promise Eli I'd fix it up a bit. But I wasn't expecting you all so soon. As a matter of fact, I wasn't expecting you at all. Had a couple of side bets on it. I couldn't imagine any nice girl being plumb crazy enough to jump on a ship with a feller she doesn't know and come halfway around the world to live in a filthy mining camp that calls itself a town with a bunch of no-good miners, gamblers, and drunks."

"Well," Savannah said. "That about sums it all up, doesn't it?"

Eli cleared his throat. "Can you settle in the girls, Annie? I really should get up to the house."

Annie nodded. "Be glad to."

Eli said a quick good-night and hurried outside, saying that Willie Joe would bring in their luggage.

"Coward," Eden murmured.

Keeping their skirts close around them, the girls trailed up the stairs after Annie. Their quarters consisted of two long, narrow rooms with a connecting door. Their beds were straw mattresses thrown on wooden frames. Annie kicked out a miner sleeping with his boots on and sent him downstairs to sleep on the kitchen floor. "I think maybe I've got some clean sheets somewheres," she muttered, brushing off the mud he'd left on the blanket.

Suddenly Annie reached down and slipped off

her boot in one swift motion. She winged it across the room, where it hit the wall with a loud smack. "Got 'im!" she crowed.

"I think I'm going to faint," Henrietta said.

CHAPTER TWELVE
The Brides Decide to Stay

Savannah woke with an uneasy feeling. She opened her eyes and saw a pitched ceiling inches from her face. A spider made his lazy way across it. The boarding house, she remembered with a groan.

She flopped over in bed and almost jumped out of her skin. A boy was perched on the porch roof outside, staring inside the window at her. He had only wisps of a beard, but the hair that was there managed to be spotted with wet patches of tobacco-stained saliva. His glazed eyes were trained on her breasts.

Savannah screamed.

The girls bolted upright in their beds. "What is it now?" Henrietta shrieked. "Indians?"

Savannah threw off her blanket and bounded out of bed. She threw up the sash and grasped two dirty wrists. Wrenching his fingers off the sill, she pushed the boy with all her strength. He flew backward and slid down the porch roof.

"Sweet Jesus!" he screamed. Then, with a howl, he landed with a splat in the knee-deep mud.

"Serves you right," Savannah muttered.

He rose unsteadily to his feet, then put one hand over his heart. "Will you marry me, darlin'?" he crowed.

With a snarl, Savannah banged down the window. The rest of the girls crowded in next to her. Outside, men were lined up on the sidewalks, standing knee-deep in the mud, even perched on rooftops across the street. They were all staring at the window with the same slack-jawed expression.

"Sakes alive," Mattie murmured. "Is this who we've come to marry?"

"They look frightening," Henrietta said.

"And dirty," Narcissa added with a sniff.

"Dirty is putting it kindly, I believe," Jenny said, wrinkling her nose. "They appear not to have bathed in weeks."

Adele giggled and waved. "Poor things," she whispered. "One almost feels sorry for them."

Plain Cora Webb twirled a curl around her finger. "I think they're cute."

Harriet peeked out from behind Fanny's ample form. Her thin arms were folded across her breasts. "These can't be the suitors Mr. Bullock was speaking of. He said they were respectable young men. God-fearing."

"I don't know about God-fearing," Eden said dubiously. "But I'd say they're *eager*."

"Look sharp, girls; here comes trouble," Savannah said.

Eli strode down the street, a tall young man by his side. The stranger's hair was a shade lighter than Eli's and hung to his shoulders. He was taller and brawnier, and was dressed in a well-worn pair of pants and knee-high boots.

"My, my," Eden murmured. "A mountain man."

"That must be Eli's brother, Josiah," Mattie said. "I see a resemblance."

"Must be the scowl," Savannah said.

Eli and Josiah approached the men. They couldn't catch the words, but Eli appeared to be furious. He pointed at Annie's house, then pointed off up the mountain.

"He wants them to go to work," Mattie guessed. "And it appears they're resisting."

Suddenly Josiah raised his rifle in the air and squeezed the trigger. The girls jumped at the sound of the deafening blast.

"I see the noble savage is a man of action," Eden murmured as the men sheepishly filed off.

Eli trudged over to the window. He gestured irritably, and Savannah threw open the sash.

"You didn't help matters much up there," Eli bellowed. "Standing around in your skivvies."

"We're perfectly decent," Savannah replied haughtily, even as the rest of the girls scurried away from the window. "It's not our fault you can't control your men. Speaking of which, can you stop inside for a moment, Mr. Bullock? We have many things to discuss." Eli started to reply, but she banged down the window.

"We really have to ask you all to be discreet," Eli began. He stood in the middle of the parlor and looked sternly at the brides. "These men haven't had much female companionship in—"

"Mr. Bullock," Savannah interrupted. "I hardly think it's your job to lecture us." She folded her arms and faced him. "Especially since you have cheated us."

Eli looked surprised. "Cheated you?"

"Just look at this place!" Savannah burst out. "You talked about libraries and opera houses and fancy teas. You said Last Chance was the most beautiful town in California. It's a mudhole!"

"The mud does surprise me," Eli said, frowning. "The rainy season isn't until November."

"We *do* have a library," Eli's brother, Josiah, added. "We had eight books, last count."

"Eight?" Eli said, turning to his brother. "You've doubled the collection."

Josiah shrugged modestly. "Well—"

Savannah stamped her foot. She saw with satisfaction that she had splashed a little tobacco juice onto Eli's trousers. "Listen to me, Elijah Bullock! You tricked us!"

"Last Chance isn't exactly how you described it, Mr. Bullock," Mattie said.

"It's ugly," Adele said.

"And the young men . . ." Jenny shuddered.

"You spoke of a paradise," Ivy said. "It seems we've landed in an inferno instead."

"And the boardinghouse!" Fanny said. "You said Annie Friend was a respectable lady! I saw her *spit* last night!"

"We want you to abide by the terms of your agreement," Mattie said. "We want to go home."

"Even Maine was better than this," Ivy said.

"All right, ladies," Eli said. "I'll abide by the terms of our agreement."

The girls nodded to each other in satisfaction.

"In six months, I'll arrange transport for anyone who wants to go," Eli said.

"Six months!" Narcissa cried.

"But—," Fanny started.

Eli held up a hand. "The Bullocks promised to transport you home, yes. But we can't afford to pay for the sea route twice. Do you have any idea how much a steamship, two clipperships, a railroad, and hotel accommodations in Panama City cost?"

"*Hotel?*" Savannah snorted. "That wasn't a hotel; it was a slum with a sign on the door."

"It was the best accommodation I could get," Eli said quietly. "No, anyone returning has to take the overland route."

"Well, we'll go that way, then," Adele said.

"You can't," Eli said. "It's too late in the year.

Snow will start falling in the mountains soon. I wouldn't allow you to risk your lives. I'm responsible for your safety."

"So we're stuck here," Jenny said.

"I'm afraid that is so, Miss Scarborough," Eli said gently. "But I assure you that my family will do everything in our power to see that you are comfortable and happy."

His tone certainly had changed from ice to honey, Savannah fumed. Despite being engaged, Eli seemed to have a soft spot for the fragile Jenny.

"Now," Eli said, turning to them. "If we're all agreed—"

"Not quite," Savannah interrupted. "Your lack of character, Mr. Bullock, comes as no surprise to some of us." She gave Eli a scornful look.

"Therefore, we expected that we might have to remain in Last Chance for a period of time," Savannah continued. "But if we are consigned to purgatory here, we have a few simple requests."

Eli looked at Josiah. He shrugged. "All right. What are they?"

"Feather mattresses and new blankets."

Eli and Josiah looked at each other. "Feather beds?" Eli asked incredulously. "For all of you?"

"Without proper rest, it's so difficult to be cheerful, don't you agree?" Savannah purred. "And without decent bedding, we could catch our deaths this winter. I'd hate for your miners to be . . . frustrated at being unable to call on us."

The implied threat caused Eli's face to turn almost purple. "Agreed," he said in a strangled voice.

"And we would like a proper door on the house. With a doorknob. Brass."

"And a knocker," Fanny added.

"What's the matter with Annie's door?" Eli asked irritably. "It keeps out the cold."

"I beg to differ, Mr. Bullock," Savannah replied. "It does not. Not to mention it's more fitting for a shack than a house. Which brings me to our other requests. We'd like a stove upstairs in both rooms for heat. No more poker games in the kitchen. And, oh, we'd like the shutters and the front porch painted. We were thinking white with green trim."

Josiah cleared his throat. "Annie's not going to like this at all."

"We'll leave Annie's cooperation to you two gentlemen," Savannah replied sweetly.

"Anything else?" Eli asked sardonically.

She gave an eloquent glance at the floor. "No tobacco spitting in the house. Now I think that's all." She sat down and folded her hands in her lap. She'd done the best she could. The brides would just have to make the best of it. Because as soon as she could arrange it, she was hightailing it out of this swamp and heading for San Francisco.

Eli and Josiah held a silent communication.

"Agreed," they said together.

They stood. Eli said his "good day" with icy politeness. He and Josiah grabbed their hats and bolted. As soon as they heard the front door close, the girls let out a collective sigh.

"Thank you, Savannah," Mattie said, her eyes twinkling. "That was masterly."

"I'm ready for breakfast," Fanny declared. "Do you think that Annie creature has any eggs?"

Mattie lifted her hand and frowned at the grime on her fingers. "We've got to take soap and water to this place."

"But that's Annie's job," Narcissa objected. "We didn't come here to be maids."

Mattie dusted off her hands. "I, for one, am not going to live in a tobacco-stained barn for the next six months."

"Mattie's right," Ivy said. "We can have this place spic and span in no time."

"Well, I'm not going to do anything without breakfast," Fanny grumbled.

Mattie laughed. "Come on, Fan. Let's see what we can rustle up."

The girls filed out toward the kitchen. Eden hung back a moment with Savannah.

"You were pretty hard on our Eli," she murmured.

"He deserved it," Savannah grumbled. "He painted a picture of paradise. Him with his fine talk of the most beautiful town on earth."

Eden chuckled. "Don't you get it, Savannah?"

"Get what?"

Eden took her by the shoulders and pushed her to the front window. "Look."

Savannah gazed out the window. This time, she didn't look at the muddy street or the ramshackle buildings. From their position on a hill, she could look clear across the town to a sweep of pine trees marching up a mountain. She could just make out a tumble of waterfall. The bluest sky she'd ever seen hit her like a blow.

Eden smiled. "You see? He didn't lie to us at all. He sees what he wants to see, Savannah. For Eli, this *is* the best place on earth. He's not the evil villain you paint him as."

Savannah grimaced. She had to admit that Eden had seen something she hadn't. Eli hadn't lied. And at least something was important to him: this land.

"So whatever happened with you two, anyway?" Eden asked, breaking into her thoughts.

"What do you mean?" Savannah asked.

Eden shrugged. "I've seen him looking at you when you're not looking at him. And I've seen you looking at him when he's not looking at you. But you don't have to tell me you're sweet on him if you don't want."

Savannah snorted. "I despise him."

"Ah," Eden said. "So you *are* sweet on him."

"I just *said*—"

"I heard you," Eden said composedly. "Funny thing about Eli," she mused. "He doesn't act like an engaged man, somehow. His eyes are a little too wandering, if you ask me."

Exasperated, Savannah turned away. Annie barreled into the parlor, removing a dirty apron. "Eli gone?"

"He left a few minutes ago," Eden said.

"Darn," Annie said. "I was going to ask him why he corralled a gaggle of princesses instead of regular folk. They called my house filthy!"

"Well, Annie," Eden said hesitantly, "you have to understand that some of the brides are accustomed to, well, more refined surroundings."

"Refined?" Annie hooted. "Well, good luck to 'em in Last Chance. They'll be the only ones."

"What about Mr. Bullock's sweetheart?" Savannah asked. She was dying to know what Eli's fiancée was like. She'd even accept Annie's judgment.

Annie looked blank. "Eli's what?" Then comprehension dawned, and she threw back her head and laughed. "He don't have a sweetheart! That was a scheme he cooked up with his brother. They figured if the brides thought he was taken, they'd be less likely to run after him. He was about to be cooped up with 'em for two months, after all."

Annie walked off, still chuckling. "That'll be the

day. I'd like to see what Caroline Bullock would have to say about that."

Savannah turned to Eden furiously. "He's not a villain!" she spat out. "He's worse!"

"What's worse?" Eden asked.

"He's a *conceited* villain," Savannah cried.

"Mmm," Eden agreed. "And he's also something else."

Savannah's eyes glinted. She couldn't wait to hear what dastardly name Eden would dream up for him. "What?" she asked.

"Free," Eden pointed out calmly.

CHAPTER THIRTEEN
SOCIAL GRACES

The brides were resting upstairs from the exhausting ordeal of cleaning Annie's house when Annie stomped upstairs.

"Mrs. Caroline Bullock is here to see you all," Annie said. "She asked me to announce her, so I'm doing it. The old copperhead is coiled on the settee in the parlor. Let me know when you want me to suck out the poison."

Annie turned without another word and banged shut the door.

They trailed downstairs to find Caroline Bullock waiting for them in the parlor. She sat, her feet planted firmly on Annie's planked floor, her narrow hands encased in tight kid gloves clasped in her lap. Her maroon skirts flowed to the tips of very small feet.

With a bright blue gaze oddly like her son's, she raked over the assembled girls. She seemed to note every frayed collar, every slight tear in lace cuffs, every splotch of mud on every hem.

"My sons informed me of your arrival," she said. "I'm happy to welcome you to Last Chance. I hope to get to know each of you in time. It is my hope that you'll assist me in my endeavor to make Last Chance a beacon of grace, culture, and refinement."

Savannah felt a poke in her back. It was Eden. She had to admit that the vision of muddy, ramshackle Last Chance as a beacon of refinement was an amusing one.

"We hope to assist you in all your efforts, Mrs. Bullock," Jenny Scarborough said in her quiet way.

Mrs. Bullock nodded at Jenny approvingly. "Now. I'm here to issue an invitation. In order for you young girls to meet the rest of the town, I will be giving a social on Friday evening, at the Bullock home."

"That does sound lovely, Mrs. Bullock," Mattie said.

"Yes. Now, due to the fact that the Bullock family has sponsored you, I feel I'm entitled to lay down a few rules."

The girls exchanged glances, but no one felt sufficiently brave to object. Savannah felt another sharp poke in her back. She stepped on Eden's foot.

"First of all, I expect modest dress," Mrs. Bullock said. "I shouldn't have to say that, but in my experience with young girls, it is better to be frank from the start. The social will begin *promptly* at eight o'clock. Only light refreshments will be served, so eat a good supper. I don't want any fainting! I don't like delicate girls. No girl shall dance with a partner who has not procured a formal introduction. No exceptions! And no girl will leave the rooms alone with a man. You will all be escorted home by my sons—no one is to walk out with a man she has just met. Is all this clear, ladies?"

Eden snorted, but she turned it into a cough. Mrs. Bullock fixed her keen blue eyes on her, and Eden flashed her sweetest smile. "I think you'll find that any concerns you might have about us will be laid to rest by our most discreet behavior, Mrs. Bullock," she cooed.

The Bullock mansion was the grandest structure in town. It was of solid brick, but unlike the other buildings, it was whitewashed. It had iron shutters painted black and a double door with, as Fanny noted, a bright brass knocker. A row of four white columns marched in a stately fashion across the wide front porch. If the girls had wondered just how powerful the Bullock family truly was, their doubts were eliminated by the sight of the impressive home.

They rustled inside the front door, nervously fingering jewelry and curls. All the brides had turned out except for Opal, who had stayed at Annie's, pleading a headache.

Inside, candles burned and banks of greenery lined the long front hall leading to the ballroom.

Only Caroline Bullock, Savannah decided as she swept into the beautiful room, would have the necessary iron-jawed belief in Last Chance's future to have built a grand ballroom.

The Bullocks had hired a small orchestra from Sacramento. As the strains of a waltz came to Savannah's ears, her heart suddenly gave a leap.

"Look at the fellows," Dottie Barbee breathed. "They shaved!"

"They're clean!" Adele said approvingly.

"I doubt their manners have improved," Georgina Temple said.

"Look at the one on the end," Fanny said. "He's quite handsome."

"I like the red-haired one in the rear," Cora Webb said with a giggle.

"The big one is staring at me," Hen fussed. "Goodness gracious me. He must be seven feet tall."

Eden fluttered her fan. "I do believe someone is about to ask me to dance."

"No, Eden," Jenny warned. "Mrs. Bullock said we must be formally introduced first."

"I've already broken the modesty rule," Eden said, smoothing her gown of green striped silk. The bodice dipped a scandalous few inches too low, revealing an expanse of Eden's perfect white skin. "Why should I listen to that old hen?"

"Maybe because she's the mother of a handsome mountain man," Savannah murmured in her ear.

As if on cue, the Bullock sons entered the ball-room. They were dressed in evening clothes with starched white shirts, their hair carefully combed, their boots shining.

"Oh, my," Narcissa breathed.

"You took the words right out of my mouth," Eden said. She stared at Josiah and swallowed.

Savannah was doing some quick swallowing of her own. She hated the way her heart picked up when Eli walked in the room. Surely her heart should have mercy on her.

Across the ballroom, Josiah nudged his brother. "Ma is heading this way," he said.

Keeping the pleasant expression on his face, Eli said, "She's probably already picked out our partners for the first dance."

Josiah gave a low groan. "What do you say we—"

"Most assuredly," Eli said.

The two brothers wheeled and started across the ballroom. Eli saw Savannah's shining hair above that sumptuous blue velvet gown that had spilled out on the deck of the ship. It looked much better on the female form, he decided.

He crossed to her side and bowed. "May I have the pleasure of this dance, Miss Brown?"

She looked surprised, but she nodded. She stepped into his arms. Her scent came to him again, rising up from her hair and her skin, and he had to close his eyes for a moment to get control of himself.

She leaned back in his arms. "I declare, Mr. Bullock, you are looking almost respectable this evening."

His mouth quirked. "I made the attempt."

"I suppose your fiancée will be proud to have such a handsome partner at the social," Savannah continued sweetly. She deepened her accent and fluttered her eyelashes. "I am just panting to meet her."

Eli looked uncomfortable. "Actually, Miss Brown, my engagement has been . . . called off."

"How devastating. I do hope your heart hasn't been smashed into little bits. People can be *so* inconsiderate when it comes to feelings, can't they?"

She took every opportunity to taunt him, and he deserved it, he thought in despair.

"Miss Brown—Savannah—I have always regretted—"

"What happened, I know," Savannah said airily. "But you're a such a man of the world that I am sure you'll recover."

Savannah regretted her quick words when she looked into his eyes. He wasn't teasing her now, she saw. He looked . . . well, seriously unhappy.

Embarrassed, she looked over his shoulder. Caroline Bullock was scanning the room, and she signaled to Josiah. Her son pretended not to see her. To Savannah's surprise, Josiah bowed to Eden and danced her away.

"Your brother appears to have a favorite," she

observed to Eli. It was time to change the subject.

"Josiah doesn't have favorites," Eli replied with a smile. "He's the most . . . disinterested person I know. Steak, chicken, or porridge, it's all the same to him as long as his belly is full."

"What a charming analogy," Savannah said. "Comparing a woman to a meal. You do say the sweetest things, Mr. Bullock."

"I didn't mean—," Eli said, embarrassed.

"I wonder what category I would fall into," Savannah mused. "Steak or chicken? If steak, would I be rare? If chicken, would I be fried or a fricassee? Or am I simply humble porridge?"

Eli suppressed a groan. "Could you do me a favor, Miss Brown?"

"You know I would do whatever is in my power, Mr. Bullock," she answered. There was just the faintest hint of mockery in her words.

"Can we . . . not talk? Can we just . . . dance?"

"I didn't realize my conversation was—" But Savannah's words died in her throat, for he had tightened his arms so that her head almost rested against his shoulder. He held her much too tightly.

Pressed against him, she couldn't help remembering that still, hot night. She remembered his hungry kisses and how his hands had roamed freely over her body.

Suddenly he stiffened. Savannah twisted her head to see what he was looking at. Eden had pushed Josiah away and was stalking across the ballroom in a swirl of green-and-yellow satin.

She was angry, Savannah saw. Her eyes blazed as she crossed the ballroom and stopped in front of the unattached men. Hands on her hips, she surveyed them silently. Some stared back boldly, others shuffled their feet, unused to a woman's brazen examination.

She held out her hand to the tall, handsome miner with the look of frank approval on his face.

Savannah heard Caroline behind her. "This is completely against the rules!" she sputtered.

Eden signaled something to the band, and they burst into a loud and energetic polka. She stepped into the man's arms with a winsome smile. She gathered up her long skirt with one hand, displaying a shocking amount of ankle, and was whirled away while the rest of the dancers stopped and stared. Eden tilted back her head and let loose a merry laugh.

Something seemed to break loose then. Something about Eden's roaring laugh and the way her partner whirled her about in the polka, something about her low-cut dress and the glimpse of too much sensual enjoyment, sent the men reeling.

They charged in one raging group toward the brides at the other end of the floor. While the band happily swung into another fast polka, hands were snatched, waists were grabbed, and girls were clasped tightly as the room exploded with the laughter of the men, the shrieks of the girls, and the sudden, happy bray of the fiddle let loose from proper waltzes. The dignified social turned into a rip-roaring jamboree. And over the din came the sound of Eden's delighted laughter.

At three in the morning, Abel Bullock paid off the band and ordered everyone out. He was tired and wanted to go to bed.

The guests spilled out into the cold air. There wasn't a cloud in the sky and the stars glimmered like diamonds.

Eden wrapped her cloak tighter around her as she hurried to catch up to Savannah. "I haven't been to such a good party in ages," she said.

"You were the one who kicked it to life," Savannah said. "Why did you push Josiah away?"

Eden's face darkened. "Josiah Bullock is a double-dealing varmint. He didn't ask me to dance for the fun of it. Eli told him about my little harmless card playing on the ship. He was asking me about my background. I've known Boston police sergeants who used more finesse."

"He was questioning you?"

"Browbeating is more like it. And all the time thinking he was being subtle!" Eden snorted. "Anyway, it doesn't matter because something wonderful happened tonight."

"What?" Savannah asked reluctantly. Why was

95

she always getting into conversations with this girl?

"I found a game," Eden replied dreamily. "For extremely high stakes, I hear. There's just one thing I'm lacking. A stake."

"That seems a necessary ingredient," Savannah said. Her feet hurt, and she couldn't wait to climb into her warm bed.

"And that's where you come in, Savannah."

"Me?" Savannah asked uneasily.

"I need your two hundred dollars," Eden said in a rush. "I can make it back, easy, and more. I'll give you ten cents on the dollar—fifteen—"

"How do you know I have two hundred dollars?" Savannah asked, aghast.

"Well, for jiminy's sake, Savannah, I've got eyes," Eden said. "What kind of gambler would I be if I didn't pay attention? You keep it under your mattress. Very unimaginative."

Savannah stopped short. "I don't believe this."

"Listen to me, Savannah," Eden said. "I've beaten the best players in New York, Boston, Baltimore, and Philadelphia, not to mention London and Dublin and . . . well, everywhere. I can double our money—"

"*Our* money?" Savannah asked, enraged.

"Well, your money, then," Eden replied, waving a hand at the technicality. "Don't you want to get to San Francisco? How far are you going to get on two hundred dollars?"

"No, Eden," Savannah said firmly. "It's the only money I have in the world."

"I don't think you understand, Savannah," Eden said mildly. "I told you I'd ask you for something someday. This is it."

CHAPTER FOURTEEN
The Pitfalls of Poker

"Let's start out easy," Eden said, shuffling. "Five card stud with a nickel open. Three bet roof, fifteen cents on an open pair and the last card. Acceptable, gentlemen?"

The players nodded, charmed by the sight of someone so young and pretty trying to play with the boys. And the way her small hands shuffled the deck! She could barely hold the cards. They would take it easy on the adorable Miss Moran.

Eden caught her teeth on her smooth lower lip. She lowered her eyes, pretending to concentrate on shuffling. She'd learned how to palm a card when she was six years old, but it never hurt to pretend a little awkwardness.

She didn't need to cheat, not anymore. She relied on a combination of luck, a mystical belief in the cards, and a knowledge of how often and how easily men underestimated her. Added to all this was the expert coaching of Black Jack Moran, the most notorious gambler in Ireland and London, and the beloved father who'd left her flat busted in Boston with a hotel bill and a debt to Crazy Eye Billy McGee.

Eden won easily on a low pair and warned herself to slow down. She giggled girlishly as she raked in the money. "I didn't realize it would be so easy to beat you fellows," she teased. They burst into delighted laughter. It was a pleasure, for now, to lose to such a pretty face.

She'd lose the next hand, and the next. Somewhere around midnight, the game would get serious. Then she'd clean them out.

From her position at a corner table, Savannah watched with a face of stone. Eden had only agreed to let her come if she agreed not to bat an eyelash. Of course, Eden had added, if Savannah wanted to show a little ankle once in a while to divert the players' attention, she wouldn't object in the least.

She'd probably lose whatever reputation she had if anyone discovered she'd even stepped foot in a saloon, Savannah knew. Luckily, most of the players were from out of town and they were using the private back room of the Fool's Rush Saloon.

Eden had pointed out logically that Savannah wasn't making sense. What did their reputations matter if they didn't want to get married? And weren't they blowing this town for the lights of San Francisco?

The risk was worth it, for Eden had promised that they would split her winnings. The pot at this table could sometimes go as high as thirty thousand dollars in a night.

As the game wore on, Savannah began to daydream. What if Eden won, say, ten thousand? That was five thousand dollars to make a start in San Francisco. By midnight, as Eden raked in her second large pot, Savannah had raised her hopes to ten thousand, all to herself.

"I'm going to have to get a glass of water," Eden said, flushing prettily. "Savannah, honey, could you please fetch me some?"

Behind the men's backs, Savannah shook her head energetically at Eden. Go into the saloon? Bad enough she was in the back room. But Eden shot her a look that meant business; Savannah sighed and went out.

She slipped inside the main room of the saloon. Roaring on weekends, on a rainy Monday night it was quiet. Savannah sidled up to the bar.

She glanced in the mirror and refastened the top button of her dress. There was no need to flash flesh like a barmaid, even if she was playing the part at the moment. She caught a flicker of movement in the mirror. Her heart stopped as Eli Bullock raised his glass in a salute.

Savannah bit her lip and prayed he'd stay in his seat. She signaled the bartender and asked for a pitcher of water. Eli picked up his glass and ambled across the room. Quickly, Savannah grabbed the tray with the pitcher on it. She darted toward the back.

But he cut her off at the entrance to the back hallway.

"Good evening, Mr. Bullock," Savannah said with great composure.

"Don't tell me you've become a barmaid, Miss Brown," he said. He clucked his tongue. "And here I thought my family was providing every luxury for the brides."

She ignored his comment. "I didn't see you as the type to frequent this type of place," she said archly.

"I always come by for a glass of refreshment after I do the payroll," Eli said, unconcerned. "It's my reward." His eyes flicked over her. "Just a piece of advice, Miss Brown, if you don't mind my being forward. If you're going to tend bar, I'd get a more fetching dress. Gray wool all buttoned up won't get you many tips."

"Thank you for the advice," she shot back. "I'm flattered that you'd take such an interest in my activities. Now, if you'll excuse me—"

She inched by him and stalked down the hallway. She heard him behind her, but she ignored him and shouldered open the door to the private room.

She tried to shut it behind her, but he only stopped the closing door with his hand, smiled, and walked in.

She plunked the tray down on the table, where

the gamblers were intent on their cards. She retreated to her corner and sat down. Eli perched on a windowsill across the room, his long legs crossed carelessly at the ankle in front of him. But Savannah knew the pose was a smoke screen. His blue eyes scanned the scene with a keen gaze.

Lose this hand, Eden, Savannah pleaded. *Just this one.*

"Three of a kind," Eden said, displaying her cards. The men let out groans. One threw down his cards in disgust. Eden's grin wobbled a bit when she saw Eli, but she greeted him casually. "Care to join the game, Eli?"

He shook his head amiably. "Rather watch for a spell, if you don't mind."

He stayed for four hands. Eden won every one. The pile of cash in front of her doubled. Now the men appeared strained. Eden hummed a tune as she raked in another pot.

Eli stood, bowed to Savannah, and left. She leaned back in her chair with a sigh of relief. Why was she afraid of him, anyway? Eden wasn't doing anything illegal. Just a friendly game of poker . . .

It was past two in the morning. Savannah's chin jerked as she slid into sleep. She pillowed her head on her arms and watched the game through half-closed eyes. *Five thousand dollars . . . ten thousand . . . twenty thousand . . . I'll start out with a suite at the very best hotel. . . .*

"Evening, gentlemen, miss," a familiar voice broke into Savannah's hazy dreams. "Heard there was a game going on. Mind if I take a chair?"

Savannah woke with a start. Annie Friend was pulling out a chair at the table. A cigar was clamped between her stained teeth, which were bared in a smile. She locked eyes with Eden.

"Sure, Annie," Eden said softly. "Deal her in, boys."

The tall, lanky miner at the end of the table, the one with the steadfast grin no matter how much he lost, picked up the cards. "Always glad to play with Poker Annie," he said.

It was all over by four A.M. Savannah felt a hand touch her shoulder, and she awoke. She raised her eyebrows quizzically at Eden, but the girl only gave a short shake of her head. "Come on. The air will wake you up."

Annie stayed behind "for a last hand with the boys." The two girls headed out into the cold night air.

Savannah shivered as she wrapped her cloak more tightly around her. "How much do we have left?" she asked warily. It couldn't be too bad. Eden looked quite cheerful.

Eden tilted her head back and looked up at the dark sky. "You think they have more stars out here than back East? Sure seems like it."

"How much do we have left, Eden?" Savannah asked. Suddenly she felt wide awake.

"That Annie must have run a few skin games in her time," Eden said.

"Skin games?"

"Card playing," Eden answered carelessly. "Of the crooked sort, that is."

"She cheated?" Savannah cried.

"Nah," Eden said. "We were watching each other too close. But she sure can play, that Annie Friend. All I'm saying is that she's a pro, that's all. Probably earned her living playing poker for a spell, like me."

Savannah grabbed Eden's elbow and pulled her to a stop. "How—much—did—we—lose?" she demanded through gritted teeth.

"All of it," Eden admitted cheerfully. "Plus my earbobs. I'll try to win 'em back next week—"

Her legs gave way, and with a *whoosh* of skirts, Savannah sank down on the muddy boards in front of the general store. She looked out at the moonlit street lined with shabby buildings, the alleys filled with garbage, the sunken roofs and peeling paint.

"So we're stuck here," she said in disbelief.

Eden sank down next her. "Guess that's why they call it Last Chance," she said cheerfully.

CHAPTER FIFTEEN
TEATIME

Word spread of the poker party like a brushfire. The brides were shocked to hear that Eden and Savannah had actually crossed the threshold of the Fool's Rush Saloon. That Eden had played until four o'clock in the morning. That Savannah had gone along.

Though there was no change in how Mattie, Ivy, and sweet Jenny Scarborough treated them, Savannah detected a slight chill from the other girls. And Narcissa and Harriet Hawke were positively icy. Eden and Savannah, they whispered, had sullied the reputations of all the brides. How would they find good men to marry them now?

Even at the moment, as they sat in the parlor with tea and cakes, the usually chattering girls had lapsed into an awkward silence. Harriet fingered the Bible in her lap in a conspicuous way. Narcissa passed the plate of cakes to an unusually subdued Dottie Barbee.

Savannah had always been a rule breaker, so she didn't care . . . too much. Eden didn't care at all.

"You know," Eden said, breaking the silence, "despite what's been whispered behind my back, I do think that Savannah's and my little escapade—"

"Escapade!" Harriet snorted.

"Now, Harriet, dear," Jenny murmured.

"—escapade," Eden repeated firmly, "has actually *increased* the brides' popularity. Why, the parlor is jammed every evening with gentleman callers." Eden bit into a muffin delicately. "If you really think about it, Narcissa, you should be thanking me instead of not offering me the strawberry jam."

Narcissa choked on her tea. "I hardly think—"

"That's right," Eden said sweetly. "You hardly do, do you?"

Harriet gasped. Jenny sighed. And Mattie pushed the strawberry jam toward Eden. Though Ivy tried to start a conversation, within minutes every bride had drained her teacup and left the room.

Savannah sighed. She knew she was about to break her rule about never again encouraging conversation with Eden. "Why must you make matters worse, for heaven's sake?"

Eden shrugged. "I'm not here to make friends," she said. "Especially with the likes of Narcissa Pratt and that prissy Harriet."

"So what are you here for, then?" Savannah asked, annoyed.

Eden ate a spoonful of jam from the pot. "Dear me. I haven't a clue. I jumped aboard back in New

York one step ahead of the sheriff."

Savannah groaned. "I see now why you've been able to turn me into a penniless outcast."

"You're not an outcast, and why should you care what Narcissa thinks?" Eden asked curiously. "Mattie and Ivy are still talking to you. And I'm sure Mary Alice would talk to us if she wasn't so shy. And even though Fanny is trying to act above it all, she's dying to hear all about the saloon. So is Dottie. They'll all come around, eventually."

"I suppose," Savannah said. But the truth was, she hadn't been worrying about the brides.

The truth was, she was thinking of Eli. She couldn't forget the look on his face when he saw her in the saloon. He'd been shocked, of course. But he'd also looked disappointed, and that hurt worst of all. She didn't know why having Mr. Eli Bullock's good opinion was suddenly so desperately important to her. But it was.

In the Bullock Mining office, Josiah pushed a steaming mug of tea toward his brother. "It's good news and bad news," he said. "Our next shipment is going to be over fifty thousand. That means—"

"Right," Eli said. "Caleb's laid up. And Willie Joe—"

"—is just one man," Josiah said. "'Course, he's worth ten. But still—"

Eli nodded as he tapped the thick rim of his

mug. As usual, the two brothers didn't need to finish their sentences.

Sometimes the biggest problem with taking gold out of a mine was getting it to a bank. The Bullock brothers had developed a system. Usually they broke up shipments into two or three to minimize the loss if the gold got stolen. Willie Joe was one of their regular carriers. Though everyone thought Willie Joe only carried passengers and freight to the city, he often secretly took gold and brought back cash to the Bullocks.

There was a good reason for the brothers' caution. There were plenty of desperadoes in the Sierra looking for quick money. Willie Joe was six foot seven inches of solid muscle, a crack shot with his rifle, and even more deadly with the long black whip he carried. The Bullocks would have trusted him with their lives as well as their gold.

"We could use guards," Eli mused. "But it might attract the wrong kind of attention. Every robber within fifty miles will know about it."

"So we use Willie Joe," Josiah said. "We hire some guns to go with him. But—"

"—we keep it low-key," Eli finished. "We don't want the word to get out."

Decision made, Josiah propped his feet up on Eli's desk. He took a gulp of the steaming tea. "Any more news on the brides?" he asked.

"I ordered the door," Eli said. "And I lined up a couple of men to paint the shutters on Saturday. It wasn't hard to find volunteers. The feather beds should be coming next week." Eli smacked his hand down on the bill for the paint from Yancy's Hardware. "I'd say Annie was the one making out on this deal."

"She deserves something for her trouble," Josiah said. "She helped us out with the poker game. Speaking of which, any trouble from those two?"

Eli shook his head. "Annie says they're flat broke. Can't get into a poker game without anteing up. Besides, Annie says they had a falling out after the game. That'll cut down on their mischief."

"It's that Eden Moran that bears watching," Josiah said, squinting out the window into the distance. "Do you know, she told me that her father was a duke? If he's a duke, I'm a . . . prince."

"They both bear watching," Eli said gloomily. "Annie told me that Eden was ahead by about five thousand the other night. Those fools she was playing with couldn't afford to lose that much. Lemuel Cray had bet his house and his horse, for Pete's sake. And didn't little Miss Moran take it from him, sweet as you please."

"Was she cheating?" Josiah asked.

"Annie's not sure. But she *is* sure that the young lady is a cardsharp from way back."

"Takes one to know one, I guess," Josiah said. "Eli—"

"I know, Josiah," Eli said.

The Bullock brothers had just made another decision. Even the most attentive eavesdropper would not have realized that the two had decided to keep an eye on the two girls.

"You should take Savannah Brown, I reckon," Josiah said. "I'll take that Eden."

A smile suddenly flashed across Josiah's face, transforming his features. Josiah's smiles were seldom, but they were impressive.

"Ma won't like this," he said. "She'll think we're courting them."

An answering mirth lit Eli's blue eyes. The two brothers grinned at each other for a long minute. They'd been bedeviling their mother since they were born, and they weren't old enough yet not to get a kick out of it.

Eli drained his tea and stood. "Just take it easy, brother. I have a feeling that girl is five foot two inches of trouble."

"Likewise, brother," Josiah said. "But in your case, I'd say about five foot six."

CHAPTER SIXTEEN
A California Necktie Party

Savannah sat by the window, frowning at the dress she was attempting to mend. It was her favorite everyday dress, blue cashmere with black braiding. She had torn the skirt near the hem.

She wanted to have it done by this evening. Eli might call. He had dropped by three times last week and twice this week. And tonight was Saturday night, when the parlor was crowded and Fanny's beau Isaac Noonan brought his fiddle.

Savannah stabbed into the material. She'd never had to mend her own dresses. She'd never even had to fix her own hair. Under her breath, she cursed at the stubborn needle. It never seemed to go smoothly in and out the way she'd seen it do in Jenny's hands.

But it wasn't the needle that was giving her trouble, Savannah admitted. It was Eli. Yes, he came to call. But was he calling on *her*? Sometimes she thought yes, sometimes no. He never complimented her or flattered her. And he never flirted at all.

Narcissa had let her know that Mrs. Bullock had

invited Jenny into her sewing circle. It was common knowledge in Last Chance that Jenny, daughter of a judge, was Mrs. Bullock's first choice for a wife for her son Eli.

The needle poked through the braid and straight into Savannah's finger. "Blast!" she exclaimed, and sucked on her sore finger.

"You look as if you could use a hand," Opal said, her voice amused.

"Bless you," Savannah said, handing her the material. She watched as Opal settled herself and began to repair the rend. It was odd to see Opal doing a task for her again.

She didn't see much of the girl nowadays. Opal usually took her tea in the kitchen with Annie. And she didn't gather with the other girls in the evenings. She stayed in her room and read. Savannah imagined that she felt out of place with the other girls. And some of them didn't help matters. They treated Opal with condescension or, when it came to Narcissa, veiled contempt. And they were Northerners!

"I'm glad to have a moment alone with you," Opal said, keeping her eyes on the work in her lap.

"I am as well," Savannah said. "How are you finding your situation here?"

"I like it well enough," Opal said.

"I see that Willie Joe is courting you," Savannah remarked.

"Do you?" Opal asked quietly. "Even though he never comes through the front door?"

Willie Joe had come to call on Opal many times, but they did their courting in the kitchen. Although Mattie had urged the couple to join the rest of them in the parlor, Willie Joe claimed that the kitchen was warmer and Opal was prone to colds. Everyone knew the real reason was that Narcissa had objected to sharing her parlor with a black man who drove a wagon.

"We're all expecting you to be the first bride to the altar," Savannah teased.

"Because Willie Joe happens to be the only other African in town?" Opal remarked dryly. "Am I bound to mate with him for that reason?"

"That wasn't what I meant," Savannah said. "I only meant that he seems a good man." Embarrassed, she decided to change the subject. "Have you located your sister in San Francisco?"

"I've sent letters," Opal said. Her face did not reveal anything to Savannah: not pain, not longing, not disappointment. "No replies. I'll have to go there myself to search. It will take some time." Opal held up the skirt to inspect it.

"How will you arrange it?" Savannah asked.

"Willie Joe said he'd take me in his wagon as many times as I wanted," Opal said. "He knows I set great store by Ruby. And he has a cousin with a rooming house where I could stay."

"That's kind of him."

"But I don't want to accept, you see," Opal said. The needle faltered, then resumed. "If I'm not going to marry him, it wouldn't be fair to take advantage of him that way."

"But he'd be helping you out of kindness, I'm sure," Savannah said.

"It wouldn't be right just the same," Opal said. She bit off the thread and held up the dress. "There. You hardly notice the tear."

"Thank you, Opal." Savannah took the dress and smoothed it in her lap. "And I wish you luck finding Ruby."

"That's why I wanted to speak with you," Opal said. She fixed her large, light brown eyes on Savannah's face. "I need something from you that's a little harder to give than good wishes. I promised my mamma I'd find Ruby. I need money to do it. I'd pay you back just as soon as I could. I'm thinking of taking in washing—"

"Opal, I can't help you," Savannah said. "I'm real sorry, but I can't. I don't have any money."

Opal's lovely face was like a mask. "If you don't want to give me the money, that's one thing, Miss Shel—Savannah," she said stiffly. "Lord knows it's yours to give or not. But you don't have to lie to me."

"I'm not lying," Savannah said.

Opal made an impatient gesture. "I know your

mamma gave you wedding money. I've seen your purse on the train, and you couldn't have spent all that money by now—"

"I didn't," Savannah said. "I gave it to Eden. You heard about the poker game, didn't you? That was my money she lost."

"But you and Eden aren't even friends," Opal said. "Why would you give her all your money? You're just refusing for the pleasure of refusing me. It's the first time I can see your daddy in you, Miss Shelby."

Savannah gasped. "Opal, you may have cause to hate my family," she said, her voice shaking. "There are times, God help me, that I—I hate them, too. But I would never refuse you something you needed if I had it to give."

Opal stood. It was plain by her expression that she didn't believe Savannah. "All right," she said quietly. "I'll find my own way."

Mattie burst into the parlor with her usual crackling energy. "Are you coming to the necktie party?" she asked Savannah and Opal.

"The what?" Savannah asked, still shaky from her conversation with Opal.

"Henrietta heard about it from Big Jake," Mattie explained. "It's an old frontier custom, Annie says. We've been sewing neckties all morning out of scraps of material. Will you come? It's a beautiful day, and it's in Jackson's Meadow."

"Thank you, but I think I'll be staying home," Opal said. "I have a letter to write."

"You'll come, won't you, Savannah?" Mattie asked. She gave her a sly look. "I'm sure Mr. Bullock will be there."

"That's hardly a reason to go," Savannah said. "But it is a beautiful day. . . ."

Annie's buckboard wagon jounced over the meadow. They felt the strong rays of the sun on their backs and could smell the grass and earth. The sky looked immense over the expanse of open land.

"There they are," Mattie said, clucking to the horse. To the left, under a stand of trees, they could see a group of men and horses.

Adele shaded her eyes. "I don't recognize anyone," she said.

"That's because you're nearsighted and too vain to wear spectacles," Narcissa said.

"They're all standing around the one on the horse," Dottie observed. "My, he has a head of red hair. I can see it from here."

"Is he handsome?" Cora asked.

"Can you see who it is, Mattie?" Fanny asked.

Mattie shook her auburn curls. "I don't recognize him at all. He doesn't look like any of the fellows we know."

"Are we sure this is where the party is?" shy Mary Alice asked meekly. "I think we should go home."

"It doesn't look very festive," Georgina said. "I'm sure we're in the wrong place."

Suddenly Mattie's hand fluttered to her heart. "Saints preserve us," she breathed.

"What, Mattie? Are you all right?" Ivy leaned forward to touch her sister's arm.

But Savannah followed Mattie's gaze. Now she could see that the man on the horse had a rope around his neck. The other end was looped around a tree branch.

"Oh, Lord," she whispered. "They're going to lynch him."

The wagon bumped over the grass. Mattie pulled on the reins, and they stopped a few feet away from the unfamiliar men.

"I think you'd better turn around, missy," the one closest to them, the one cradling a rifle, said. "We're conducting private business here."

"*Illegal* business, I'd warrant," Mattie said. Savannah marveled at her calm, clear tone. With deliberate slowness, she set the brake.

The man with the rifle stepped forward. "Come on, ladies. Enough of this foolishness."

"It's you who appear to be foolish," Savannah said. She tried to sound as calm as Mattie. "We have jails and judges in this county. We're not barbarians. We believe in the law."

Savannah turned her eyes away from the man on the horse. He was not the handsome bandit out of the storybooks. He was dirty and mean-looking. Not someone she'd be tempted to save under the best of circumstances. But she had to help Mattie. The other girls seemed paralyzed. Only Ivy was sitting straight, her eyes blazing, gripping Mattie's arm in a show of solidarity. If only Eden were here! The girl had spunk, at least.

The rifleman's eyes glinted at her, pure steel. "We believe in the law, too. Frontier law. And we aim to follow it."

"We got plenty of trees," someone spoke up. "We could hang 'em all."

"Don't be a fool, Hank," the man with the steel-gray eyes said. "Let's just get this over with. Ladies, you are welcome to watch."

Silently, gracefully, Jenny slid onto the floor of the wagon in a faint.

Mattie spoke to Savannah out of the corner of her mouth. "What should we do? We just can't let them hang him."

Savannah swallowed. One of the men secured the end of the rope to the nearby tree. As soon as they kicked the horse out from under the red-headed man, he would swing free and break his neck. . . .

"There's more of us than there are of them," Savannah murmured. She glanced in back of the wagon at a prostrate Jenny. "Well, almost."

"Let's charge 'em," Ivy said.

Savannah glanced at Ivy in admiration. She'd

always thought Mattie was the strong one of the two girls. Ivy, with her sweet smile and her tragically broken heart, had always been too pallid to interest her.

"You two sure have guts," she murmured to them. "For Yankees."

"Come on, girls," Mattie urged. "On the count of three, jump out of the wagon and charge."

"*What?*" Narcissa asked.

"One," Mattie muttered.

"Do ya want a blindfold, Red?" a man called.

"Two—"

"Nah. I want to see yer ugly yellow faces as I die," Red responded calmly.

"*Three!*" Mattie cried.

With a whoop, she leaped out of the wagon, followed closely by Ivy. Savannah jumped after them, and the three charged the surprised men. Savannah pushed the first one, but his chest was like a wall. And suddenly she realized he was laughing and that the rest of the girls were still in the wagon.

Ivy was imprisoned by a grizzled character who held her against his chest. Mattie was sitting on the ground, the man with the rifle standing over her. Savannah felt her wrists being seized in an iron grip.

The leader of the group let out a stream of curses. "Let's do it, boys!"

Then, Savannah heard the distinct sound of a rifle being cocked behind her.

"I wouldn't do that if I were you, Quint," a familiar voice said.

She twisted around. Eli and Josiah stood to the side, their weapons drawn and leveled. They would almost look casual to an observer. But it was impossible to miss the taut purpose underneath the nonchalance.

The man with the rifle paused. "Well, if it ain't the Bullock boys," he said.

Josiah brought his other hand up. In it was a second six-shooter.

"You all know what a good shot my brother is," Eli said easily.

"Best in the county," one man said nervously.

"And his older brother's second best," another man said nervously. "I'm going home."

"You're risking your hide for this varmint?" Quint said angrily to Eli. "He stole my horses! And it wasn't the first time he'd done it, neither."

"We'll take him to Grass Valley to jail," Eli assured him quietly. "He'll be tried and punished, Quint. I promise you that."

Savannah watched Quint consider this. She marveled at the power Eli and Josiah had. They must have been at least twenty years younger than Quint.

"All right," Quint said, lowering the rifle. "You can take him. But I'm coming along with you to make sure he gets there."

"Fair enough," Eli said.

As the men untied the rope from around Red's

neck, Eli turned to the girls. "What do you all think you're doing out here?" he asked angrily.

Henrietta poked her head out of the wagon. "We were looking for the necktie party," she said. She waggled a scrap of fabric in the air. "See?"

"The . . ." Eli looked at Josiah. The two brothers burst out laughing. Every time they seemed to be in danger of stopping, a fresh attack washed over them.

"What did I say?" Henrietta asked meekly. "Mamma always said I had no sense of humor. I suppose I must, after all."

"We call lynchings necktie parties in these parts," Eli finally was able to tell them.

"That Annie," Savannah said. "She knew what she was sending us into. I bet she's having a good laugh right about now."

Josiah rubbed a hand over his stubble. "This one's going to go around the county, I reckon."

"I think Jenny's coming to," Dottie called.

The smile left Eli's face. He strode to the wagon. "Miss Scarborough! Are you all right?"

Jenny nodded. "I am embarrassed to say, Mr. Bullock, that the sight of any kind of violence is . . . extremely distressful to me."

"Has someone given her some water?" Eli barked. He jumped into the wagon and supported Jenny against his chest. "Get her some water!"

Georgina held a skin bag full of water to Jenny's shaking lips.

Savannah felt rooted to the spot. The realization thudded through her. And a fierce and terrible jealousy pierced her like a knife.

It's Jenny he wants, she thought. *It was never me at all.*

CHAPTER SEVENTEEN
NEW TACTICS

"All right," Eden said, flopping down on the sofa next to Savannah a few days later. "I know you're not talking to me. I want to know what's wrong."

"Nothing's wrong," Savannah said. "And you're right. I'm not talking to you."

Unconcerned, Eden tossed one of the apples she was holding into Savannah's lap. "Mattie told me about the necktie party."

"Yes, I suppose we're the joke of Wildcat County by now," Savannah said.

"That's not what I'm talking about." Eden lifted her skirt up to her knees so that she could cross her legs. "Don't look at me like that; I get enough of it from Narcissa Pratt. I'm sure you've seen my garters before. Now, do you know that Jenny is talking about starting a school with Ivy?"

"No," Savannah said in a small voice. "That's very . . . commendable."

"Do you know that she and Caroline Bullock are sewing a new flag for that shed they call a town hall?"

"Why are you telling me this, Eden?" Savannah asked, exasperated. "I already know that Jenny Scarborough is perfect." She took a savage bite of her apple.

"My point is not Jenny's perfection, as bloody provoking as that is," Eden replied. "My point is that Jenny is trying to *belong*. If you were Eli, which girl would you choose—the one who sews American flags with your mamma and is devoted to improving your beloved town? Or the one who looks down her nose at your home and insults you to your face whenever she can get in a good clean shot?"

"I don't know," Savannah said sulkily.

Eden waved her apple at Savannah. "Do you want to know what your problem is?"

"No. And I don't care to hear—"

"Your problem is that you're using Southern belle tactics on a man of the frontier."

"What am I supposed to do?" Savannah grumbled. "Shoot a bear? I was brought up to sit here in the parlor in my silks and be worshiped."

"Exactly my point, darlin'," Eden said. "Now you've got to get involved in building Last Chance. Isn't there anything in town that you'd like to change or improve?"

"Where should I begin?" Savannah muttered. But she sat, pondering what Eden said. She thought of row after row of boring buildings on Main Street. Room for improvement? Naturally. But what could one girl do?

Suddenly she sat up. "The Marigold Theater."

Eden was inspecting a brown spot on her apple. "The what?"

"Haven't you noticed it?" Savannah asked. "It's a perfect jewel box of a theater, sitting right in the center of town. What if we brought in an acting troupe and put on a play?"

"I love plays," Eden said. "But it wasn't exactly what I had in mind. I was thinking of something boring and virtuous, like knitting socks for the poor."

"I'm not the type to knit socks," Savannah said, chewing. "But I think I could try importing a little culture."

Eden grinned. "Well then, I guess that will have to do."

Eli was alone in his office when she knocked. He looked up in surprise when Savannah knocked and swept through the door.

She didn't wait for him to ask her to sit but plunked down in a chair opposite him. "Who owns the Marigold Theater?"

Eli's eyes were wary. "Why do you ask?"

"Because I want to know," she said.

"It's been shut for years," Eli said. "Must be gnawed to death by rats by now."

"It's in beautiful shape," Savannah said. "It just needs a good sweeping, that's all."

"Would it be too much, Miss Brown, to ask you to come to the point?"

"First of all, I want to know who owns it. Second, I want you to help me bring a theatrical troupe to Last Chance."

"I see," Eli said. He paused. "No."

"No?"

"No. I'm not a theatrical producer. I'm a businessman."

"I'm just asking for the deposit for the troupe," Savannah said. "I'll pay you back out of the proceeds. I'm sure we can fill the theater. I figure that the brides will help me clean the place up, and—"

Eli held up a hand. "The answer remains no."

This wasn't the way she'd imagined it. Eli didn't seem impressed with her community spirit at all. He seemed more . . . annoyed.

"All right, then," Savannah said. "I'll ask the owner of the theater. Surely they'll see the wonderful opportunity this is."

"The owner says no," Eli replied shortly. "My family owns the theater, and I speak for them."

"*You?*" Savannah slumped back in her chair. "Just my luck. The one person in town with absolutely no sense of fun owns the theater."

Eli looked offended. "I beg your pardon."

Oh dear, Savannah thought in despair. Now she was insulting him. She was glad Eden wasn't there to see it.

She tried another tack. "Why did your family build it in the first place, then?"

"We didn't," Eli said. "It came as part of a real estate deal. We really wanted the building next door." He gave her a meaningful look. "The last owner went broke."

"Don't you ever use it?"

Eli nodded. "Sure. Once in a while we hold auctions there for dead miners' belongings. Josiah got a real good horse at one of them—"

"Eli, didn't you promise us art and culture even though we were coming to a small town? I want to import culture to Last Chance. It's necessary for the town to thrive," Savannah said ringingly, "to join the ranks of civilization—"

"Don't you ever take no for an answer?"

"No," she said, stung. Eli was so indifferent. She didn't think he'd fall into her arms, but she *was* looking forward to a little admiration. "And I'm not leaving until you agree."

Eli sighed and carefully placed his pen back on his blotter. He came around the desk, grabbed her by the elbows, and lifted her to her feet.

"Thank you for dropping by," he said through his teeth. "So sorry you have to go."

So she had wound up in his arms at last. The fact that he was about to throw her out of his office was a tiny detail she wouldn't think about just yet.

"Are you really going to throw me out?" she asked breathlessly.

"You bet," Eli growled.

Easy for him to say. But Eli found that he couldn't move. He had her in his arms again. Of course, it wasn't under the most romantic of situations. The trouble was that romance, that nasty devil, was stealing into his heart. He desperately wanted to kiss her.

They hadn't met each other's eyes. His gaze was trained on her hairline. She was looking at the curl near his ear.

It seemed like the stupidest thing in the world to do right then, but Eli gave up and kissed her.

With the first feel of her lips against his, he knew why he'd kept his distance from her for weeks. A firestorm raced through him, and he remembered hot tropical nights and the feel of her bare skin against his hands. He remembered that he had only just stopped in time. . . .

He pulled away. "Damn."

Her lips curved. "Nicely put, Mr. Bullock. You're so—"

"Don't talk," he said, bending down toward her again for a kiss that went on and on until their legs buckled. Eli bent Savannah over the desk and buried his lips in her neck. Her hair had come loose, and he felt it against his cheek. He scraped his teeth against the softness of her throat and heard her moan.

"Eli!" Josiah's jovial voice came through the door.

Eli sprang off Savannah and moved to the door so swiftly she felt a draft. She looked down and saw that the buttons of her dress were undone. Her hair had come loose and was hanging down her back. Sinking down on the other side of the desk, Savannah tried to reassemble herself.

Eli opened the door but kept his body blocking Josiah's view.

"What's the matter with you?" Josiah asked.

"I was taking a nap," Eli said.

"A nap?" Josiah's voice was full of disbelief. Eli might have told him he'd just robbed a stagecoach.

"Did you want me?" Eli asked.

"Just came to tell you I'm heading out to the mine. Then back to Annie's for tea. Eden invited me."

"See you at dinner, then," Eli said shortly.

"But first I wanted to talk to you about this plan of ours," Josiah said, leaning against the door frame as if inclined to chat.

"Let's talk later," Eli said hurriedly.

"First off, it's asking too much of a man to have to tangle with Eden Moran. She keeps calling me uncivilized. Do you know that yesterday she asked if I knew how to use a fork?"

"Josiah—"

"I swear, Eli, I just might kill her. Look, even if the two girls are a couple of swindlers up to no good, I don't see how it's totally our responsibility. We can ask Annie to keep an eye on them. She went right on over to the poker game and cleaned Eden out when you asked her to."

Eli leaned his head against the door frame. He closed his eyes. "Can we *please* discuss this later, Josiah?"

"Sure. You do look tuckered out. Maybe you should take another nap."

Eli closed the door. He leaned his forehead against it, counted three breaths, and turned around.

Savannah stood up, buttoned, smoothed, and white to the lips. She reached for her cloak and swirled it around her shoulders.

"Listen," Eli started. "It's just that—"

She strode across the room, reared back, and hit him in the stomach with every ounce of her strength.

Gasping, doubled over, Eli had no choice but to watch as she walked out the door.

CHAPTER EIGHTEEN
THE JOYS OF SHAKESPEARE

"How was your walk?" Eden asked when Savannah banged through the door.

"Illuminating," she said. She whirled off her cloak. "I've decided two things. The first is that I'm bringing a theatrical troupe to Last Chance. And I know how I'm going to raise the money, too. We're going to have a fair in the town hall. We'll bake pies and muffins. And we'll knit things: gloves, mufflers—"

"We already have neckties," Eden pointed out dryly. "I must say, Savannah, godspeed and all that, but I think I'll still arrange to have a headache that evening. What's the second thing you decided?"

Savannah's eyes blazed. "That Eli and Josiah Bullock are . . ."

"Wait, don't tell me. Two egotistical blockheads?"

"They aren't courting us, Eden," Savannah said. "They're watching us like two Pinkerton detectives. They think we're a couple of swindlers here to rook the men of Last Chance."

The smile on Eden's face faded as Savannah's words sank in.

"Bloody swine!" she cried, outraged. "I've been off the crook since I left Boston. Sure, I don't mind winning a few hands of poker, but I'm no blackleg!"

Savannah winced. Eli and Josiah had been wrong, but not that far off the mark. The truth was that Eden did have a criminal past. And she herself was hiding her own circumstances. But still, to have used soft kisses to further their own ends! It was despicable.

"Eli was the one who sent Annie to the poker table that night," she went on. "That's the reason I lost all my money."

"And my earbobs," Eden said. "And to think that I thought that Josiah—that worm!"

The clock chimed four. Mattie arrived to set up the tea table. The girls crowded behind her in the daily ritual, setting out napkins and cups.

"What are you two conspiring about?" Ivy asked, handing Savannah a napkin.

"We're going to bring theater to Last Chance," Savannah said. "And we're going to have a fair at the town hall to pay for it."

"And I'm going to sell kisses at it for five dollars apiece," Eden announced.

A hushed silence fell over the girls.

"Eden, you can't," Dottie pleaded, a blush stealing over her plump cheeks. "It would make you appear to be . . . a bad woman."

"No one will marry you, Eden," Hen said.

"Mrs. Bullock will be scandalized," Harriet said.

A catlike smile played over Eden's lips. "Ten dollars," she said. "And I'll give them their money's worth, too."

Eden wore red. Her gown of satin brocade was cut low, and the bodice showed off her slender waist. When she leaned forward to purse her pretty mouth, she revealed inches of creamy bosom nestled into black lace.

The line at her booth was the longest at the fair.

For five cents apiece, Ivy wrote love letters for lovesick miners. Hen sold out all the neckties for a dollar each, but had to listen to necktie party jokes all evening long. Georgina and Dottie sold every treat they made. Mary Alice was too shy to man a booth, but she contributed twenty apple pies, which were auctioned off to the miners. Mary Alice nearly fainted when Doc Cavendish bought one for twenty-five dollars.

At the close of the evening, Savannah counted out the cash and coins with a satisfied air. She pushed the lid of the tin cash box shut with difficulty. They had plenty of money, more than enough to pay the troupe, buy refreshments, and print tickets. They didn't need the Bullocks at all.

"Looks like you have a success on your hands."

Savannah looked up. Eli leaned against the wall, his hands in his pockets. "Congratulations."

She gave a short nod. She hated him. She hated his lazy stance, she hated his coolness, she hated his boots.

"Who are you fixing to bring to town?" he asked, not moving from his negligent stance.

"Haven't decided yet," she replied, not looking at him. She busied herself with gathering up her shawl. "I'm going to look in the *Alta California* tonight."

"I'd advise something light," he said. "A musical, something like that. Just so long as it's not Shakespeare. I've never been able to stomach Shakespeare."

Savannah smiled at him sweetly. "Of course I shall keep your advice in mind."

That evening, she pored over the San Francisco papers in the parlor. There were a surprising number of advertisements for theatrical troupes. She ran her fingers down the boxes, wondering if the boasts were real.

After three months of a triumphant tour of the Continent . . . The most dazzling display of theatrical expertise in this century . . . Thrill to the amazing Rolanda LaVille with exotic French-accented dance imperiale . . .

But then she found it:

Alistair Sinclair Starr's Traveling Troupe of Troubadours.

It wasn't just that King Ludwig of Bavaria had pronounced them "extraordinaire!" Or that they'd even played for kings and queens. What caught Savannah's eye was a more humble boast:

We specialize in the greatest Thespian marvel of all time: Mr. Wm. Shakespeare!

CHAPTER NINETEEN
MR. VALENTINE

On the afternoon of the show, Savannah headed out to greet Starr's Traveling Troupe of Troubadours. They had parked their bright blue-and-gold caravan by the river.

She was glad to leave Annie's boardinghouse. The brides were all in shrieks and flutters over the elegant evening ahead. Everyone had escorts, and most were going to the Mountain View Hotel for dinner. Narcissa and Jenny had been invited by Caroline to the Bullock mansion for an early supper before the show.

The sound of the rushing river told her she was close. Savannah ducked under the trees and started toward the caravan, visible underneath a tall pine. She nearly stumbled on a man resting against a tree.

He sprang to his feet. "Terribly sorry. Are you all right, miss?"

He was possibly the handsomest man she'd ever seen, Savannah thought dazedly. His hair was gold and thick, and it glinted in the sun. His eyes were a startling amber ringed with darker brown, and his mouth was full and sensual underneath his mustache.

"I'm fine," she said, holding out her hand. "I'm Savannah Brown. I'm the one who arranged to bring the troupe to Last Chance."

"Of course." Inclining his head, he clicked his heels. "Laertes, at your service."

"Hamlet's best friend," she said. Just about the only thing she had been able to retain from school had to do with plays.

"Precisely," he said. "Wait until you hear my Queen Mab speech."

Savannah frowned, puzzled. "But isn't Queen Mab—"

"Mercutio's speech in *Romeo and Juliet*? I'm glad to see you know your plays, Miss Brown. Yes, you're perfectly correct." He flashed a devastating grin. "But Alistair Sinclair isn't a purist. He's a borrower. He takes pieces of his favorite plays and . . . mashes them together. Very few people seem to notice."

"How extraordinary," Savannah said, smiling.

"Now, in Alistair's version of *Hamlet*, for example, Ophelia herself doesn't drown—she takes poison. She thinks Hamlet is dead, you see. But he isn't. After he rises, Polonius administers an antidote to Ophelia. They marry after all."

Savannah laughed. "And how does Laertes fare in this version?"

"He lives," he whispered. "And he marries—can you guess?"

"Not Hamlet's mother?" Savannah suggested.

"Of course!"

They burst out laughing.

"You have a lovely smile," he said.

Savannah looked down at the ground, embarrassed. It had been quite a while since someone gazed at her with such obvious admiration. Eli usually scowled when he looked at her.

"Ah, how rude of me," the young man said quickly. "I should introduce myself. Benedict Valentine, at your service."

"I'm very glad to meet you, Mr. Valentine."

"You must forgive me if I embarrassed you," Benedict said. "Actors are more used to judging faces, you see. And you, if you don't mind my saying so, have an extraordinary face, Miss Brown."

"Thank you."

"As a matter of fact, the Starr troupe could use a face like yours," he said lightly. "Our Ophelia is fifty if she's a day. Alistair lost his ingenue—his daughter got married and quit the stage. Unfortunately, his wife has taken over her role. I have a splendid idea. We're just about to have tea. I'm sure Alistair and Egberta would be delighted if you could join us."

"Thank you," Savannah said, pleased. "I'd like that very much."

She followed Benedict's elegant back down the grassy slope toward the caravan.

What an interesting life he must lead, she

thought. Traveling around the countryside in a caravan would be a much more attractive existence than scrounging for gold in a tunnel.

Benedict turned and flashed his devastating grin at her once again. As a matter of fact, what had she ever seen in Eli Bullock at all?

From an upstairs window, Savannah watched Jenny walk out on Eli's arm. Jenny looked lovely in cream-colored satin with pale pink ribbons running through lace insets in her wide skirt. Eli touched her arm to guide her into the carriage. The sense of desolation Savannah felt seemed out of all proportion to that small, polite gesture.

Jenny and Eli were followed by Josiah and Narcissa. Narcissa was practically bouncing, so happy was she to be on the arm of a Bullock brother. Her black hair crackled from the vigorous brushing she'd given it, over and over that long afternoon.

Eden's eyes narrowed. "Where's a raw egg when you need one?"

She turned and rustled away. Eden's shoulders were almost bare in her striped green silk gown. She'd altered the bodice to make it more daring. Now that Josiah was courting Narcissa, there was no need for Eden to beware of Caroline Bullock.

"They're expecting us downstairs," she told Savannah.

Savannah took a last look in the mirror. She was

wearing her blue velvet gown, but it was freshly trimmed with rose satin. Dottie had loaned her a pair of black jet earrings, and Savannah liked the way they caught the light.

She walked downstairs with Eden. In the parlor, the brides had gathered.

"There you are," Mattie said. "You two are just in time to say good-bye."

"Good-bye?" Savannah asked.

"To the first bride of Last Chance," Mattie said, smiling. "All best wishes to Opal and Willie Joe!"

Across the room, Opal stood stiffly while the brides applauded.

"She's leaving with Willie Joe for Sacramento in just a few minutes," Mattie murmured to Savannah. "They'll be married there tonight."

Savannah slipped over to Opal's side. "When did you change your mind?" she murmured.

"I didn't," Opal said shortly.

"But you're marrying him," Savannah said.

Opal turned. "You should know better than anyone, Savannah, that sometimes you just don't have another way out."

Savannah's mouth snapped shut. Opal had spoken the words without bitterness, but they burned into her heart just the same. She of all people should have known how it hurts a heart to marry someone you barely know.

And she hadn't helped at all.

Savannah's eyes filled with sudden tears. "Opal, I'm so sorry. I feel so foolish . . ."

"Why?" Opal asked. "It's not your concern."

"But you came to me for help," Savannah said. "And I didn't help you."

"You couldn't."

She couldn't then, it was true. But she'd just worked like the devil to raise money to bring a troupe to Last Chance for a play. A *play*, when this girl's life depended on a few dollars.

"If I had any money left from the fair, you know I would give it," Savannah said. "But everything was so expensive. The tickets and refreshments," she said lamely. "You know how it is."

Savannah's voice trailed off. Opal just looked at her. She had the mercy to say nothing.

"I'd best be going," she said. "Willie Joe is waiting outside."

"We'll miss you, Opal," Mattie called across the room.

"We surely will," Ivy said. A few of the other girls murmured a good-bye, but it was not an overwhelming response.

Opal showed no emotion as she looked back at all of them. "Thank you for your wishes," she said softly. "Good-bye."

"She doesn't look very happy for a bride," Harriet sniffed after the door closed behind her. "They don't feel the same as we do, you know."

"Oh, do shut up, Harriet," Savannah said fiercely. "You can be such a fool."

The lobby gleamed with polished brass, sparkling glasses, and gleaming mirrors. It was crowded with happy faces and delighted laughter, but Savannah's heart felt heavy as she made her way to her seat next to Eden. She couldn't forget Opal's quiet dignity as she walked out the door to a life she hadn't the resources to refuse.

The actors were greeted with whistles and applause and much foot-stamping from the miners. They were a vocal, easily moved audience, afraid of the ghost of Hamlet's father, appreciative of the clanking swords of the soldiers, and whistling appreciatively at Benedict's legs in tights.

But trouble started when Ophelia appeared. Expecting a slender young ingenue, the audience got fifty-year-old Egberta Starr, white powder settling into her wrinkles, and a filmy green satin gown revealing a thick waist and legs that "belong on a pian-er, by Jove!" one miner called.

For the miners, plays meant pretty girls, and they had been rooked. Murmuring escalated to catcalls, and Egberta made the mistake of freezing up at the criticism. Savannah wondered if it had anything to do with the whiskey she'd seen Egberta pouring in her teacup earlier. "For my nerves, dearie," Egberta had told her calmly.

Now Egberta forgot her lines and forgot to move. She stood, frozen, staring out at the unfriendly faces.

The first rotten tomato hit her on the knee.

CHAPTER TWENTY
LEAVING LAST CHANCE

Someone stood up and shot at the ceiling. Half the audience erupted in shrieks of fear, half in cheers. Egberta hit the floor of the stage with a wail, her skirt flying up to reveal rather stained long underwear.

Benedict calmly gathered up his sword and tunic and left the stage. Alistair dodged a rotten potato and followed, dragging Egberta behind him. Their departure seemed to have the ease of long habit.

Savannah pressed herself against her chair as the room erupted into chaos. She heard screams and gunshots and high, hysterical laughter. Escorts desperately tried to clear a path for the women in their charge. A miner jumped onto the stage and began to recite "Woodman, Spare That Tree."

From their position in the first row, Savannah and Eden looked at each other. "What now?" Savannah asked above the din.

A gunshot exploded near Eden's ear, and she flinched. "I'm taking cover," she said, darting underneath her seat.

Savannah gazed down the aisle to see if she and Eden would be able to navigate it. Through the crush of bodies, she saw Eli sweep Jenny into his arms. The girl's face was white and her eyes darted in fear. Tenderly, Eli shielded her against his chest.

He really does love her, she thought. Her heart felt barren. She backed away and hit the stage.

The voice was right by her ear. "May I rescue a damsel in distress?"

It was Benedict, kneeling on the stage, bending toward her.

"Please," she said faintly.

He reached down and put his hands around her waist. He hoisted her up and sat her on the stage in front of him.

"Backstage," he said, his words just audible over the din.

She stood. He slid his arm around her waist protectively. Then he swung the other arm to encompass the audience busily fighting, singing, and laughing.

"I know this isn't a recommendation for the life of the stage," he murmured in her ear. "Still, would you like to join us?"

She looked at him, startled.

"Alistair was taken with you at tea," he said. "Especially with how well you acted Ophelia." She had read a speech or two with Benedict, feeling silly, and thought them gracious for applauding.

Benedict winced as a miner threw a chair across

the stage. "And our audiences are letting us know that we need an ingenue."

"But I'm not an actress," she said.

He shrugged. "You have beauty and nerve. All you need is a pair of pink tights and you're more than halfway there. I'll teach you the rest. What do you say? Come with us. Tonight. We've worn out our welcome in this town—we're heading back to San Francisco. It will be a lark. Why not join us?"

She looked out over the theater. Eli had reached the exit doors. She saw Jenny's hand curl around his neck.

"Why not?" she said.

Annie's boardinghouse was thankfully deserted. Savannah packed her clothes quickly, trying to ignore the lump in her throat. This was what she wanted, wasn't it, a chance to get away to San Francisco? She would have money. She would have adventures. It was just what she wanted.

She closed her soft carpetbag and valise and looped her reticule over her arm. Turning, she saw Eden in the doorway.

"You're leaving."

Savannah nodded. "There's nothing here for me, Eden."

Eden nodded.

"I'm going with the troupe," Savannah said. "They've asked me to join them. I'm going to be an actress." She said the word shamefacedly, thinking Eden would laugh.

Eden didn't even smile. She only nodded again. "Do they have room for me?" she asked. "Just for a ride to San Francisco, I mean. I'll make my own way from there."

"I'm sure they have room," Savannah said. "But are you certain you wish to go?"

Eden shrugged. "I won my earbobs back the other night. What other reason would I have to stay?"

The city of San Francisco rose up to meet them across a gray and misty bay. To Savannah, the city looked to be a larger version of Last Chance, a collection of ramshackle buildings with sagging roofs. She was used to the grace of Southern cities, the wide avenues lined by leafy trees. San Francisco was raw and swimming in mud.

When they reached the city, Eden buttoned up her cloak with a shiver and grabbed her bags. She said her thanks to a sleepy Alistair and Egberta and motioned to Savannah to walk a little way with her.

They stood at the end of the pier, not knowing what to say.

"Well, good luck to you, Savannah," Eden finally said. "And remember, I'm still going to pay you back that money someday."

Savannah nodded. She wondered why she felt so close to tears. Half the time she wondered if she liked Eden at all. "What will you do?" she asked.

Eden shrugged. "I'll make my way. Thinking I could give up my old life—that was a dream. I'll do just fine."

Eden looked like a child, her hat shading her delicate, tired face. Impulsively, Savannah reached for her. They hugged, holding each other close for a moment. "Godspeed," Eden whispered.

She stepped back and bumped straight into Benedict. "I'm sorry," she said, laughing and reaching out to steady him. "You'll watch out for her, won't you?"

"I shall," Benedict promised.

Savannah stood beside him as they watched the small figure walk away. The bright green feather in her hat waved at them as she retreated. Soon the fog swallowed her completely.

Alistair came up to them, squinting through the mist. "Well, I'll be going. Bertie's asleep in the wagon. The rest of the troupe already took off." He held out a hand for Benedict to shake. "You keep in touch, Ben. I might be having work for you and the miss any day now. Things are looking up."

"I'll be in touch," Benedict promised.

Alistair touched his hat, gave a final polite leer at Savannah, and trudged back to the wagon.

"I don't understand," Savannah said. "Don't we have another engagement?"

"Not yet," Benedict said. When he saw her crestfallen face, he patted her shoulder. "Don't fret, now. This is an actor's life. It won't be but a few days, probably."

"But what will we do?" Savannah asked nervously. "Where will we go?"

Benedict shivered. "First off, to a restaurant, I think. I could do with some coffee. Then, we'll get a couple of rooms at a hotel I know. Hot running water and clean sheets. How does that sound?"

It sounded very good indeed, but Savannah hesitated. Had she been foolish to agree to come with Benedict? Had he made a certain assumption about her character?

He flashed a grin. "I know what you're thinking, and you can put the thought away. I don't have designs on you, my lovely. We're comrades. Fellow actors waiting for our break." He tugged her cloak closer to her neck in a brotherly gesture. "Shall we start with coffee? That will fix you up, won't it?"

The fog was thick and wet, clinging to her hair and clothes in tiny droplets. She was tired from the long journey and wet through to the bone.

She smiled into Benedict's warm amber eyes. "Right now, Benedict, a pot of hot coffee sounds like salvation."

CHAPTER TWENTY-ONE
In Which the Bullock Brothers
Make a Startling Discovery

Elijah and Josiah sat in their office, not speaking. For once, they were not communicating silently. They were not coming up with two plans that, when spoken aloud, would be exactly alike.

For the first time in their lives, the news was so bad that they couldn't think at all.

Fifty thousand dollars worth of gold was missing. Stolen. Gone in the night while the town was filled with revelry, dancing in the streets, and hosting a marksmanship contest that had riddled Mayor Chester Allen's opera hat with holes. Fortunately, Chester had not been conscious at the time.

Finally, Eli broke the long silence.

"First off," Eli said, "we don't tell Pa."

"I was thinking the same," Josiah said. "There's no need to, yet. The only ones who know are you, me, and Dale because he opened the office this morning."

"Second, we find whoever took it and get it back," Eli said.

Josiah nodded. "That's the best way."

"Have any suspects in mind?" Eli asked. His voice sounded offhand, casual, and he glanced out the window as he spoke.

"I surely do," Josiah said.

There was another pause. This time, the brothers *were* thinking. Thinking of soft lips and teasing eyes. Tiny waists and sharp tongues and gleaming hair.

"They took us for fools, Eli," Josiah said.

"We don't know it was them," Eli said.

"They're both gone," Josiah said.

"That's true," Eli agreed.

"Gone without notice," Josiah said. "Didn't tell anyone they were going. Left a note for Annie saying thank you."

"Mmm," Eli said. "Still—"

"Who else?" Josiah asked.

"I was thinking Red Fontaine," Eli said. "Nate Kennedy came over from Grass Valley for the show last night. Said Red escaped from jail. Could have been him."

"He's no friend of ours," Josiah agreed. "Even if we did save him from a stretched neck."

"We did put him in jail, though," Eli said. "And you won't mind if I point out that he is a thief."

"So's that Eden Moran," Josiah said. "Something's wrong with those two leaving like that, Eli. I can feel it in my bones."

Eli sighed. "Let's split up, then. I'll go to San

Francisco and look for the girls. You find Red. He'd have gone over the mountains, most likely. You're a better tracker than I am."

A slight smile teased Josiah's dour mouth. "How come you always get to chase the pretty girls?"

Eli grinned. "Because I'm better-looking."

Josiah stretched his long legs out in front of him. "So. What story can we come up with to throw Pa off the scent?"

"I don't think we'll need a story," Eli said.

"We always need a story, Eli," Josiah said.

"Not this time," Abel Bullock said behind him.

Bull-necked, barrel-chested, he filled the doorway with bulk and fury. "When were you boys fixing on telling me?"

"We have it under control, Pa," Eli said. "We don't want to get the marshal involved. Josiah and I have a few ideas as to who could have done it."

"Where in the Sam Hill have you boys been all morning?" Abel bellowed. "They already know who done it. A posse already rounded them up and brought 'em back."

Eli and Josiah sprang to their feet. "They're here? In Last Chance?"

"Bringing them in now," Abel said. "Look."

They hurried to the window. Below, down the hill, they could see the main street of town. Men on horseback were brandishing long poles. A couple slowly walked between them, stumbling from exhaustion. One of the men leaned over to prod the woman on the back of the legs.

"Lord help us," Eli said.

It was Opal and Willie Joe.

CHAPTER TWENTY-TWO
LOGIC AND NEW BONNETS

At lunchtime, the dining room of San Francisco's Imperial Hotel was crowded with diners. Prosperous businessmen, beautiful women, visitors from the East, distinguished Europeans. Savannah kept twisting, trying to see it all.

"Benedict," she whispered, "just look at the plumes on that hat!"

He looked up from his plate of oysters. "Very becoming."

"Not too vulgar?" Savannah asked.

Benedict slid an oyster into his mouth. "Not at all," he answered. "You should have a bonnet like that, Savannah. As a matter of fact, the one you have is hideous. It looks as though it's been round the Horn."

"It's my best bonnet," Savannah said defensively. "And it's only been through Panama," she added.

Benedict burst out laughing. He had an infectious laugh, and a few ladies looked over at him. They smiled at his handsomeness, and their companions glowered. Benedict winked at Savannah; he always noticed when people looked at him.

She had been in San Francisco for only two days, and Last Chance had receded like a disagreeable dream. Benedict had advanced her money to pay for her room and board, insisting that she could pay him back when she was the toast of the town. When she protested at the extravagant hotel, he waved away her objections. And when she told him she felt certain the whole situation was dreadfully improper, he told her that actors were bored by propriety and it was time she learned how to live.

"Your clothes are too plain, as well," Benedict continued. "That dress, for instance. Appalling."

"But it's my best everyday dress!" Savannah protested, smoothing her hand over the cashmere.

Benedict took a sip of coffee. "Why a beautiful girl wants to sit there in a drab wool dress buttoned up to the neck when there are silks and satins to be had is beyond me. You're going to be an actress. You can't dress like a lady."

Savannah's eyes grew wider at his words. Benedict said the most appalling, delightful things. No one had ever told her that she shouldn't dress like a lady before.

Benedict squeezed lemon juice over his oyster. "Directly after lunch, I am going to buy you a new bonnet."

She leaned over to whisper to him. "You can't buy

me clothing, Benedict, it's dreadfully improper. You talked me into the hotel, and I'm very grateful, but clothing . . . I just *can't*. Just because I've slipped a bit doesn't mean I have to slide down the hill altogether."

"Eat your food, pumpkin," Benedict said. "If it bothers you, then we'll just look. I promise."

Eli closed the door of the rooming house behind him. He tucked his wallet into his pocket. He was twenty dollars poorer and no closer to finding Savannah and Eden. His only lead had fizzled out.

Annie had told him that she thought the girls might have hitched a ride to the city with the theatrical troupe. Alistair Sinclair Starr had been charming—after he ascertained that Eli wasn't there to get back the deposit. He remembered both Savannah and Eden after a gold piece was pressed into his hand.

Eli walked down Green Street, struggling to contain his fury. The only piece of valuable information Alistair had given him was that he believed Savannah and Benedict Valentine were . . . together. He saw them say good-bye to the slender pretty young one after they got off the ferry.

Benedict. He remembered the man. He'd literally bumped into him in the saloon that day, where Eli had gone for a cup of coffee. The man had been too handsome for his own good. And charming! He'd even talked to Eli about mining.

He stepped into a restaurant for lunch. Over his sandwich, he considered the situation, trying to use Josiah's logic. He desperately needed a cool head at the moment. Right now he wanted to buy a rifle and blow a large hole through a very blond actor.

He had to have a place to start. San Francisco was no longer the sleepy Spanish town of Yerba Buena it had been before the gold rush. It was a bustling, hustling city with countless hotels, rooming houses, and apartments. He couldn't very well roam the streets, hoping for a glimpse of one of the girls.

By the time Eli had finished his lunch, his head was cool enough to come up with the logical approach Josiah would applaud: When tracking an animal, stake out their lair. He would look for Eden first.

Benedict stopped at the hotel desk for the key. Savannah hung back. She always felt embarrassed when Benedict picked up the keys. And this afternoon, she was carrying a large hatbox from Renée's Millinery Salon. She was sure the hotel desk clerk would misinterpret the situation.

Benedict had been so charming and so insistent. He'd told her that if she wanted to audition in a few weeks, after they'd rehearsed, she'd need to look like an actress. And Madame Renée had not been at all shocked that a man who wasn't her husband was buying her a hat. She assured her that here in San Francisco, gentlemen bought ladies bonnets all the time. She'd go out of business if it weren't so!

Besides, she had always had trouble with being a lady. The role had never fit properly.

Savannah realized that Benedict wasn't his usual merry self. She saw his hands clench behind his back as he leaned closer to the desk clerk.

She took a few steps closer and heard the desk clerk clearly.

"Yes sir, I'm positive. A man was asking for you earlier. And the young lady as well. No, he didn't leave his card. He said he would return. He asked for your room number—"

"You didn't give it to him!"

"No, of course not. Would you like to leave a message for the gentleman, should he call again?"

"No message," Benedict said in a choked voice, and walked away.

Savannah hurried to catch up with him. "Benedict, who is it?"

"I have no idea," he said. "No one knows I'm here. Did you tell anyone?"

"No," Savannah said. "Of course not. But why would someone be looking for you?"

Benedict shrugged. "I have a few debts, nothing serious . . . perhaps it's that. The clerk said he thought it was a detective, though he wasn't sure."

"A detective?" Savannah asked weakly. "Oh dear. Oh, Benedict. I'm so sorry to bring you into my troubles."

He took her arm and pulled her into a curtained alcove. "What are you talking about?"

Quickly, Savannah spilled out her story. She should have known that her father would never give up. He and Justus had mostly likely hired a private detective to find her. She wouldn't be too hard to trail, she supposed. If Opal had figured it out, a detective probably could.

"Do you mean to tell me that your father would hire someone to track you thousands of miles?" Benedict asked doubtfully.

"You don't know him," she said with a shiver.

"Well, I'll be . . ." Benedict laughed. "You're being followed."

"I suppose this could mean trouble for you," Savannah said meekly. "I'm so terribly sorry, Benedict."

He stroked her cheek absently. "Don't fret, pumpkin. I'll take care of it. This hotel is too public, anyway. I know a better place. Somewhere more discreet. We'll pack and leave right now."

"You'd do that for me?"

He smiled. "The actor's creed, remember? We take care of each other. Come, we don't have a moment to lose. I'll hide you away, my precious, where no one will ever find you."

CHAPTER TWENTY-THREE
MRS. BENEDICT VALENTINE

As dawn was breaking Eli found Eden Moran in the back room of a dingy saloon near the waterfront.

She sat at the table, her dark hair down and curled around her creamy shoulders. An unlit cheroot was clenched between her white teeth. She made a low noise in her throat as she swept the biggest pot of the night into her lap.

"That's it for me, gentlemen," she said with her usual arch sweetness. "I'm afraid to say that I really must bid you good-night."

Eli stepped forward. "Not quite yet, I'm afraid."

Sensing trouble from the tall, rangy stranger, the rest of the gamblers threw down their cards and hurried out the door.

Casually, Eden stuffed the bills into a small velvet purse. "Mr. Bullock, what a pleasant surprise," she drawled. Rising lazily, she gave him her hand. "I'm always glad to see old friends. Is your . . . brother with you?"

"No," Eli said. "Is your friend with you?"

"Savannah? No, we parted company upon our arrival."

Eli kicked out a chair and sat on it, astride. He looked up at her coolly. "Give me one good reason why I shouldn't call a policeman right now and throw your larcenous soul in jail."

"You bet," Eden replied warily. "Because I haven't broken the law."

Eli smashed the table with his fist. A few men looked over, but it was late, and they weren't inclined for a fight that wasn't their business. They turned back to their conversation.

"I want the gold back," he said fiercely.

Eden looked sincerely puzzled. "Gold?"

"The gold you stole from Bullock Mining," Eli said, spitting out the words. "After we fed and sheltered you for months. You're a couple of cold-hearted swindlers, you and that Savannah Brown, or whatever her name is—"

"Someone stole your gold?" Eden blurted.

"You're good," Eli said. "I'll give you that."

"I won't dispute that, Eli," Eden said. "I *am* good. At poker. Even, I admit, pickpocketing at one time. But—"

"Pickpocketing?" he said. "My pocket was picked sometime that day. The keys to the office and the safe were on a ring."

Eden rolled her eyes. "What an idiotic place to keep keys to a safe."

Eli glared at her. "You just admitted you were a pickpocket."

Eden sat down with a sigh. "I'm tired, Eli. Worn out, in fact. Look. I didn't steal your money. Neither did Savannah. She left Last Chance without a penny to her name. We both did."

"Why did you leave so suddenly?" he asked.

She met his gaze coolly. "We had our reasons." Eden took a breath and, relenting, sat back down. She leaned across the table and spoke softly.

"Eli, you spent weeks and weeks and weeks with us. Savannah and I might have secrets. And maybe we're not the most well-mannered or virtuous girls in the world. But surely you know that we'd never steal from you and Josiah."

Eli felt paralyzed. He sat astride the flimsy chair, staring blankly at Eden. The cunning expression that was usually on her face was gone. She looked softer, he thought. Kind.

She leaned over and touched his hand. "Poor Eli. You wanted to think we did it, didn't you?"

He didn't answer. She was right. She was right, and now, sitting here in this filthy barroom, he knew she wasn't lying. Eden and Savannah hadn't stolen the money. He rested his chin on his hands and sighed.

"I don't know if Josiah will believe it or not," he said.

"Where is Josiah?" Eden asked casually.

"He's tracking Red Fontaine," Eli answered. "He's our other suspect. He escaped from jail in Grass Valley."

Eden put her hands on her hips. "Do you mean to tell me, Eli Bullock, that a known thief escaped from jail and you suspected two young *girls* of taking it?"

"You're not exactly innocent, Eden," Eli said tiredly. "So don't get all indignant on me."

"So what now?" she asked. "Are you going back to Last Chance?"

"I still have to find Savannah," he said.

"Why?" Eden asked. "I thought you believed me when I said we didn't steal your gold."

"I've still got to find her," Eli said doggedly. "Josiah won't let me back in town if I don't look in her face and hear her tell me she didn't steal it. Where is she, Eden?"

"I don't know," she said.

"But you know *something*," Eli guessed.

"Maybe I do," Eden said. "But I'm not going to help you without a price."

Eli groaned. "I thought so. I don't have much left, thanks to tracking you through every gambling parlor in San Francisco—"

"It's not money I'm wanting, dearie," Eden said in her lilting way. "It's a confession."

"What confession?" he asked suspiciously.

She cocked her head. "Tell me you love her."

Eli squirmed in his chair. "Love who?"

"Tell me you love her," Eden repeated impatiently. "Why do you think you traveled all this way, for heaven's sake? Why do you think you have to find her now? Josiah will believe you if you tell him we didn't do it."

Eli's mouth set stubbornly.

Eden stood and picked up her velvet bag. She looped it over her wrist, then picked up her cloak. "It was nice seeing you, Mr. Bullock."

"I don't want to love her!" he burst out.

She laughed wickedly. "I know. But you do."

"I do," he snarled.

Eden sat down primly. "That's better. Now, there's just one other thing before I tell you. You have to promise me something."

He groaned. "A confession *and* a promise? That wasn't our deal."

"I know," Eden said, frowning prettily. "It's unfair of me, but I just thought of it. You can't tell your brother that I picked Benedict Valentine's pocket. Josiah has such a bad opinion of me already. And I wouldn't have done it if I wasn't desperate."

"I won't tell Josiah, Eden," Eli said. "I promise. What did you find out?"

"I only got a dollar anyway," Eden grumbled. "I think he keeps his money elsewhere. Smart weasel. I should have gone for the watch . . ."

"Eden—"

"All right, all right, I'm coming to it. He also had a piece of paper in the wallet. With a name and address on it. It could be a place to start—"

Eli grabbed her hand. "Let's go."

Benedict returned to the room with newspapers, a loaf of bread, and some cheese.

"Filthy day out there," he said. Their new room was a far cry from the Imperial Hotel. It was too warm, and the stove in the corner smoked. Savannah closed her eyes for a minute, remembering cold, crisp morning walks in the mountains, the smell of pine, the snow crunching under her boots . . .

"Pass me the bread, will you?"

She tossed the loaf to Ben and leafed through the newspaper. Suddenly she sat up with a cry.

"Saints preserve us!"

He looked up, alarmed. "What is it?"

Savannah scanned the article in the paper. "The Bullock Mining Company was robbed!" she said.

"Let me see that," he said, rising.

"And they think Opal and Willie Joe did it," Savannah said, aghast.

Benedict stopped. "Who?"

"Opal," she said, reading quickly. "She came with me from Georgia. She was a slave on my father's plantation. Willie Joe is her husband."

"They caught two Africans?" Benedict said, sitting down again. "Well, I'll be."

"They're afraid of vigilantes," Savannah said, still reading. "They're afraid that folks won't wait for the trial and they'll string up Willie Joe. Could that really happen, Benedict?"

He shrugged. "It's been known to. A couple of years ago they dragged Charles Cora right out of jail and hanged him for shooting Marshal Richardson. Right here in San Francisco."

"And they're going to send Opal back to my father's plantation!" Savannah cried. "This is dreadful. We have to go back."

Benedict looked up from cutting some bread, nicking his finger with the knife. He licked his wound. "Go back?" he asked, amused.

Savannah began to pick up items from the bureau. "I have to help her."

Benedict rose and put his hands on her shoulders. "You must be joking. Why go back to that quagmire to help two black thieves?"

Savannah twisted away. "Because I know they didn't steal that money. And I also know she's a free woman. They can't send her back. Let me go, Benedict! I understand if you want to stay here. I can go myself."

His hands tightened on her shoulders. "You're not going anywhere."

"Don't be silly, Benedict, of course I am." She tried to shake him off, annoyed.

"No," Benedict said. "You're not."

She felt the heat of his breath. Suddenly, his honey-colored eyes looked hard.

"Ben?" she asked waveringly.

He ran his hands up her arms. "How can you go," he murmured, "when we haven't gotten to know each other yet?"

She almost laughed. "Benedict, what are you doing?"

But he bent over and she felt his hot, wet mouth against her neck. "What you've been wanting, darling."

She pushed him. "Don't be a goose, Ben—"

"Don't make fun of me!" he suddenly thundered. He held up an index finger in front of her face. "Don't *ever* make fun of me," he spit into her face.

She backed away and hit the dresser. "All right," she said soothingly. "Just calm down."

He grabbed her again and pressed his lips against hers. "You want this," he growled against her mouth. "And God knows I've paid for it."

"You said the money was a loan," she whispered.

"Of course I said that; gentlemen always say that . . ." Benedict gave a chilling smile. "You really didn't know, did you? You didn't realize that I'd compromised you. Precious, we're living together. Haven't you noticed?"

She saw with horror that he was only telling the truth. And now she was trapped.

"Don't even think about looking for help here,"

Benedict said. "This place doesn't have the kind of clientele who would respond to a lady in distress."

Savannah brought up her foot and crashed it back down again on Benedict. He'd taken off his muddy boots, and the heel of her shoe caught him on his instep. He dropped her arms and howled.

She shoved him with all her strength, and he went over. When she jumped over him, he caught her ankle, and she crashed to the floor. He tried to drag her backward, but she hung on to the leg of the bed.

But he was stronger than she was. He jerked her backward, and the bed was too flimsy to hold her. She held on, however, and dragged it along with her.

He released her ankle long enough to wiggle on top of her. His face was buried in her skirts, and he laughed as she tried to twist away.

She let go of the bed and flailed behind her, trying to hit him. But her arms were too short. His hands came up and slid underneath her body to cup her breasts. She screamed, but her mouth was against the floor, and she was almost out of breath. The sound she made wouldn't penetrate the door, she knew with mounting desperation.

She needed something to hit him with. Moving the bed had revealed something underneath it— Ben's carpetbag.

One hand still on her breast, he slid up her body.

With the other hand, he was trying to lift her skirts.

She threw out her hand and grabbed the handle of the bag. He might have something in it, something to threaten him with . . .

The bag was so heavy. She slid it toward her. His hand was tearing at her drawers now.

She reached inside. Her fingers slid along something cold and hard—metal. She grabbed it and pulled.

Benedict removed his hand from squeezing her breast. He fumbled at his trousers. He had her pinned with his weight, and his movements were driving the breath from her body.

It was a box. A strongbox. And stenciled across it were the words BULLOCK MINING COMPANY.

"You did it," she breathed.

He grunted and ripped her drawers. Savannah screamed and flailed behind her, but she couldn't land a blow.

It seemed as part of the dream, but the door flew open. She saw, impossibly, Eden's pretty face, shocked and furious. And Eli, his face grim, standing there, looking down at them.

Eli didn't get a chance to move before Eden was on top of Benedict, fighting like a wildcat. Roaring, he got to his knees, Eden on his back. Savannah twisted away. She picked up the metal strongbox, lifted it over her head, and crashed it down on Benedict.

He groaned and lay still.

There was a pause that stretched out into several long seconds.

"So much for rescuing you ladies," Eli said in a conversational tone.

Curls hanging in front of her eyes, a long scratch down one cheek, Eden started to laugh. Savannah leaned against the bed, bodice torn, drawers around her ankles, and laughed, too.

Eli squatted over Benedict. "He'll live," he said.

"He stole your money," Savannah said.

Eli nodded. He couldn't take his eyes off her. "Are you all right?" he asked softly.

She nodded and started to cry.

"I think I'll go see about sending for the authorities," Eden said, heading for the door.

Eli crouched until he was facing Savannah. He handed her his handkerchief. She couldn't quite meet his eyes.

"Look at me," he said gently.

She looked at him obediently. "What?" she whispered. "Are you going to yell at me?"

He laughed gently. "No. Savannah—"

A commotion outside in the hall made him pause. They heard Eden, her voice sharp, angry, telling someone not to go inside, not just yet, and who did he think he was, anyway—

But the door flew open. A tall man with soft gray eyes took in the unconscious man on the floor and Savannah in torn drawers.

"What in blazes is going on here?"

Eli looked at Savannah. "Do you know this guy?"

"I'm afraid I do," Savannah said weakly. "He's my husband."

CHAPTER TWENTY-FOUR
LOVERS AND GAMBLERS

It was not the most congenial trip back to Last Chance. A glowering Eli didn't say a word. A bewildered Justus stayed silent. Savannah decided that talking would only make matters worse, seeing that the man she loved was furious at her, and her husband had every reason to despise her. Even the normally talkative Eden was cowed.

"I just came along so they wouldn't kill you," she whispered to Savannah.

"Just don't desert me now," she replied, with an uneasy glance at Eli.

But releasing Willie Joe from prison made everything worthwhile. The angry crowd that surrounded the jail dispersed, disappointed that a hanging would not take place after all.

With Justus by her side, it was also easy to prove that Opal Pollard was not the property of Winston Moxley Bruneau. Her ownership had been, in fact, transferred to Shelby Bruneau Calhoun, and thus by right to Justus Montgomery Calhoun, who agreed with his wife that Opal was free.

Slowly Savannah and Justus followed Main Street to the river. They stood watching the rushing, tumbling water for a time.

Savannah cleared her throat. "I have treated you abominably, Justus, I know—"

He took her hand. "Shelby. Please, let me speak first. When you first ran away, I was furious. And your father matched my fury and then some. We were determined to find you. We felt ourselves disgraced. If I had been able to find you in New York, I would have dragged you back to Georgia by your hair."

"And had every right to do so, I suppose," she said.

"Every legal right," Justus said. "But I've been searching a long time for you, Shelby. Even after your father had given up. And as I got farther and farther from home and everything I knew, it began to seem a poor joke on me. Why was I chasing a wife who didn't want me? Who had gone through hell to get away from me? What kind of a marriage would I have if I made her return to me?"

He looked around at the mountains. He shrugged. "I am ashamed to admit that these questions would not have occurred to me back home. Somehow things are different here."

"They certainly are," she agreed softly.

"What I'm trying to say is, I was coming to tell

you that I'll let you go. I'll grant you an annulment if you wish it. I don't see why you have to remain a fugitive all your life just because you don't want to be married to me. Your mother is worried about you. Your Aunt Ursula, too. I'm afraid your father has disowned you."

"That is no loss to me," she said bitterly. "Justus, I'm ashamed to say that once I classified you with my father. I didn't know you."

A small smile quirked his mouth. "I had a feeling you looked at me as the devil."

Savannah grinned. "I suppose I did, complete with horns and tail. But really, now that I look at you plain, I have to admit that you're rather hand-some." She put a hand on his sleeve. "And kind."

He swallowed. "I want you to know, Shelby, that I fell in love with you the first time I saw you—at that dinner party when you spilled wine on my trousers."

"Oh, Justus," Savannah said, biting her lip to stop the laughter that bubbled up inside her. She'd deliberately spilled that wine because she knew her father was angling for Justus to make an offer. "I'm so sorry."

"I entered into the marriage hoping . . . well, you can imagine what I hoped. But we can't choose whom we love, can we?"

"No," Savannah said softly. "And that is our ill fortune, isn't it?"

He smiled and touched her cheek. "It doesn't have to be. Not for all of us."

He was sitting in his office, facing the window, when she came in. He turned a face to her that betrayed nothing. Savannah almost missed the scowl.

"Opal's going to stay in Last Chance, at least for a while," she said. "Even though folks almost lynched her. Willie Joe, too. I'd say that's quite sporting of them."

Eli nodded. "I heard."

"I thought it would be good if we made them feel . . . welcome," Savannah said. "There's lots of folks in town who feel they were wronged."

"Maybe some," Eli said. "Not enough."

"I was thinking of giving them a dinner at Annie's," Savannah said. "And I was hoping you could be there. And Josiah."

He picked up a book and put it down again. "So you're staying for a while, Mrs. Calhoun?"

She nodded. "I'm staying. And I won't be Mrs. Calhoun much longer, either. Justus has agreed to an annulment." She peered at him, trying to see if this information moved him.

Eli was impassive. "I see."

"Eli, I'm sorry," she said in a rush. "But you can see, can't you, why I took a false name, and didn't tell the *complete* truth, and . . . everything?"

"Not everything," Eli said. "Not why you ridiculed my town and insulted me and never, not for one minute, acted like a reasonable person—"

"And you were such a model of gentlemanly behavior?" she said hotly. "You'd sooner . . . sooner spit in my eye than be nice to me!"

"You could have trusted me!" he yelled.

"Why?" Savannah demanded. "Did you appear to be a person who could be trusted? A person who cared? You thought I was a thief! You pretended to court me just to check up on me! And you almost . . . almost seduced me and then rejected me cruelly the next day. And you lied about having a fiancée!" she finished triumphantly.

"You were worse," Eli said with deadly calm.

She tossed her head. "Hardly." But then she tried to hide a smile. "Do me a favor," she said, coming closer to him.

"Me? Never again," Eli said.

She put her hands on his shoulders. "Don't talk," she murmured. Then she leaned down and kissed him.

Eli broke the kiss reluctantly. "We'll have to talk eventually."

"I know," Savannah said. "Eventually. And you'll have to admit that I—"

He silenced her with another kiss.

Savannah slid her arms around him. She didn't like being silenced, and she'd certainly inform Eli of that as soon as they stopped kissing. But she could tell him that . . . eventually.

From her position on the street outside, Eden saw Savannah and Eli locked in an embrace. *At last*, she thought in satisfaction. She'd never met such a blockhead as Eli Bullock, unless it was his brother, of course.

Hadn't she given Savannah advice on changing tactics once upon a time? Eden thought, turning back toward Annie's. Perhaps it was time she followed her own advice.

If she wanted Josiah—and she had to admit, as long as there was no one else around, that she did—maybe she should . . . reform. She knew he disapproved of her card playing. She knew he thought she wasn't to be trusted an inch.

Eden stopped stock still in the middle of the street. Give up poker? Why not? She could be sweet and demure and learn to knit. She could be just as ladylike as that gargoyle Narcissa Pratt.

A cart rumbled by her, and Eden sprang to get out of its way. In the mud by her feet she saw something wink at her. She picked it up and rubbed it. A twenty-dollar gold piece! Her luck was changing.

It was a sign. She could take the money and do nothing with it. She could refuse temptation and tuck it away for a rainy day.

Eden tossed the coin in the air and watched it catch the sunlight. But then again, she usually spent rainy days in bed with a book. And there was a high-stakes game in Grass Valley . . .

Experience the passion and desire of all the

BRIDES OF WILDCAT COUNTY

A sneak preview of the
next romantic adventure

Scandalous: Eden's Story

by Jude Watson

The temperature plummeted. Even with the fire, the cabin was freezing. Eden tossed and turned, trying to be quiet. She didn't want to rouse Josiah, but she was too cold to sleep.

She heard him stir. His voice was gruff when he spoke. "You'd best sleep up here. It's too cold on the floor."

She hesitated. She knew the offer was no invitation to vice. But what would he think if she accepted?

"Don't be foolish, now," Josiah said, seeming to read her thoughts. "Where will I be if you freeze to death? I'll never tell a soul we slept in the same bed, Eden. We'll never speak of it again. You have my word." He raised the blanket.

She brought her own blanket with her and slipped into bed beside him. He was dressed in long underwear and a flannel shirt, and he felt wonderfully warm. Her whole body was shaking, and he wrapped his arms around her. Pressed against his chest, she heard his heartbeat against her ear.

Heat crept through her veins as his warmth invaded her. Her cold fingers uncurled and lay against his chest. His chin rested on the top of her head, and he wrapped his arms more firmly around her.

The rumble of his voice was something she felt as well as heard. "Better?"

She nodded against his chest. "Much."

Minutes passed. She curled herself closer to him. She heard the fire crackle and the sound of his breathing.

Slowly, the trembling left her body. She relaxed against him. Her breathing slowed.

And then, something changed. Perhaps what alerted her was the sound of his heartbeat. It no longer beat steadily, reassuringly. It speeded up.

He cleared his throat. He adjusted his body so that the only part of her touching him was her cheek against his chest.

She knew then why he had retreated. She had come to his bed, comrade to comrade. But now that her flesh had warmed, she had warmed him, too.

The heat was the point. Now she was a woman and he was a man, and they were lying together in a bed.

He was holding himself stiffly now. She tilted her head back.

"Josiah, I can sleep on the floor."

"No."

She didn't want to sleep on the floor. She wanted him to kiss her. She wanted him to shrug off his notions of what being a gentleman was all about. She wanted his lips against hers, she wanted to run her hands down his arms.

"Josiah," she whispered.

"Eden, don't." He was still rigid, but his eyes were soft.

"Don't . . . what?" she asked, reaching out and running a finger down the stubble of the beard he'd grown. She let the finger trail down his throat. It eased over his Adam's apple and she watched him swallow.

"Don't . . . do . . . that," he forced out.

"What?" she asked innocently. She trailed her hand down his shoulder, slid down his waist, and came to rest cupping his hip.

"That?" she asked.

"That," he answered in a groan, and reached for her.

He brought her next to him in one swift movement and crushed his mouth against hers. She felt the roughness of his beard and the softness of his lips.

His tongue teased her lower lip, and she opened her mouth to him. They kissed, deep and long. He held her tightly against him, running his hands down her body. Somehow, the buttons of her shirt came undone and his hands slipped inside. He groaned again when he felt warm, bare skin.

She seemed to feel each sensation separately. His hard kiss, his hands against her skin, his soft hair against her fingertips, the feel of his firm body against hers.

The wool shirt slipped down her shoulders, and she was bare. She slipped her hands underneath his shirt, eager to feel his skin against her fingers. His breath was hot in her ear as her fingers traveled across smooth skin.

He turned to slide himself over her body . . .